BEVERLY HILLS KING

CALIFORNIA SUITS, BOOK SIX

CLAIRE MARTI

BEVERLY HILLS KING, California Suits, Book Six

ISBN: eBook 978-1-7372993-9-4

ISBN: Paperback 979-8-9895950-4-4

Published By: Claire Marti

Edited by: Lindsey Faber

Cover Design: Sarah Paige, The Book Cover Boutique

❀ Created with Vellum

For everyone who feel they found their true family.

In the words of Richard Bach:

*"The bond that links your true family is not one of blood,
but of respect and joy in each other."*

PROLOGUE

THE RAY-MICHAELS WEDDING RECEPTION

Monterey, California

*L*ucas Sutton leaned against the polished teak bar and sipped his whiskey, savoring the cool ocean breeze drifting in through the glass doors. The temptation to slip out to the moonlit gardens and listen to the Pacific surf crash on the shore was real. But it was his best friend's wedding, so he was trapped in the overheated noisy room for another few hours.

"Come with me, handsome. The rest of the bridal party is already dancing." Brigitte Thibault pressed one graceful hand on his arm.

Talk about temptation. His breath lodged in his throat. When he gazed down at the petite brunette, all thoughts of escape disappeared. Somehow, his mind blanked when she was around, which promised to become a major problem now she was his employee.

Her shiny dark hair was pulled back from her exquisite face, emphasizing sky-high cheekbones and enormous smoky eyes. Her off-the-shoulder lavender silk maid-of-honor gown framed delicate collarbones and an elegant neck that beckoned to him to take a bite.

"Lucas?" She said in her throaty French accent and pursed her perfect red pout.

"Sorry, yeah, um, sure. Sure we should join everybody. Let me put down my drink." And now he was stammering like the high school math geek he once was.

He'd crushed on her from afar the first time they met a few years ago, but he managed to keep his distance. Until now. He placed his glass on the bar and wiped his palms on his charcoal gray dress pants. *Get a grip.*

She caught his hand, and her citrusy floral scent surrounded him, filling his senses. They joined the guests on the dance floor, where his best friends were already dancing with their partners. Yeah, the other "Hotel Kings" had all fallen in love with their employees when opening their respective hotels.

Wagers were already flying about him and Brigitte becoming a couple next. This time around, the group would be better off betting against them hooking up. Because his focus was one hundred percent on work--no time to consider his personal life for the foreseeable future.

Besides, his new concierge was out of his league. Way the hell out of his league. Her confidence, sophistication, and vibrant energy magnified her external beauty. He could handle one dance with her without revealing just how attracted he was to her, couldn't he?

She wound her arms around his neck and grinned, mischief gleaming in her eyes. "Can you believe our best friends didn't kill each other and got married instead?"

His shoulders relaxed and he laughed. "Right? None of us could believe it when Ryan hired Charlie. Especially when we found out she'd been his nemesis back in the day."

"Oh, they couldn't stand each other. And here they are—married. I never thought I'd see Charlie picking out bridesmaid dresses and taking vows. But I'm happy for her. Happy for them." Emotion flickered behind her slate-blue eyes before her dark lashes lowered.

"Me, too." But right now, all he could feel was how perfectly she fit in his arms, her subtle curves brushing against him, the heat from her silky skin searing through him. She felt like heaven and the urge to skim his hands down her body, grip her hips, and tug her against him burned through him. He inhaled a steadying breath, struggling for self-control.

"Well, I hate to argue and besides, you could never be angry with me. I'm charming and everybody loves me." She winked and her lips curved into a teasing grin. "So, we'll have no drama in Beverly Hills."

His throat grew parched. Yeah, the woman's playful attitude was irresistible. "And here I thought you were shy and modest."

"Hmmm, shy? Not exactly but don't take anything I say too seriously, Lucas. I like to keep things light and fun, life is short, *n'est-ce pas*? We will make a wonderful team and Paramount will be the best hotel in the chain." She laughed, rose on her tiptoes, and pressed a kiss to his cheek.

And every muscle in his body hardened. If this damn dance didn't end soon, the urge to kiss her promised to overwhelm him. Was she this flirtatious with everyone or did she feel the electricity sparking between them, too?

The song ended, he released her, and stepped back. Drew in a ragged breath. A waiter appeared with champagne and

Brigitte plucked two flutes from the tray and handed him one. Her fingers brushed his and heat raced up his arm.

Brigitte tapped her glass to his, smile wide. Oblivious to his discomfort. "Let's toast to making Paramount the best, *oui?*"

"Definitely." He downed half the glass in one mouthful, savoring the icy liquid, praying it would cool him off. Hell, it was a miracle his glasses hadn't steamed up.

They joined their friends at the bar and Lucas moved to the far end. Safer that way. Brigitte entertained with stories of her and Charlie's exploits back in the day, her elegant hands waving, her eyes sparkling. Being the center of attention came as easily to her as breathing. A beacon of light and energy, her presence warmed everyone in her orbit, including him.

"Come on, single ladies, let's do this. But fair warning, I'll fight you for those flowers. I'm ready for Mr. Right." Jon, Ryan and Charlie's assistant at Pacific Jewell Inn, appeared next to them bubbling with excitement.

"Oh, I don't want that bouquet. It's all yours." Kenzie waved her champagne flute. The new Spa Manager out in Palm Springs, she worked with Austin. And yes, Lucas had bet on them being the next Hotel Kings couple.

Brigitte shook her head. "I'm never getting married. You two go."

"Don't ruin the fun. Come on." Jon dragged the two women into the center of the room where a small group was gathered waiting for Charlie to perform the traditional bouquet toss.

Brigitte stood with her arms crossed and allowed the flowers to sail past her.

And Lucas dropped firmly back to earth. Yeah, even if he had a chance with Brigitte, she'd made it clear she wasn't one for settling down. And although he'd been single a long time, he wasn't built for casual flirtations.

Better to figure it out now before they were working together every day.

CHAPTER 1

*B*everly Hills, California

ON A SUNNY SEPTEMBER MORNING, Lucas Sutton's brain exploded. Simply detonated without warning and scattered into tiny fragments. Had the big earthquake finally hit California and the incessant buzzing was the fall-out?

"Mr. Sutton, have you heard a word I've said? I am very, very, upset and I don't know if I can work in these conditions."

No, it wasn't aftershocks, it was a high-pitched whine from Dagmar——the interior designer who was supposed to be the best in Beverly Hills. Yes, Dagmar used a one-word name like Beyoncé or Cher, but this self-named solo artist lacked the harmonious vocal chords. Lucas and his Hotel Kings partners had hired her to assist with Paramount's renovation.

He was tasked with managing their fifth luxury boutique

hotel and ensuring it was as successful as the first four in their exclusive chain. No pressure.

"Which conditions?" He waved one hand around the vast unfinished space that would serve as the hotel's first impression. An active renovation site, complete with dust and tarps and equipment, of course it was a mess. A fact she'd been fully aware of before arriving this morning.

Dagmar snorted and tossed her cherry red hair extensions. "I have sketches. I have deadlines for testing out some of my design concepts and this, this place is nowhere near ready for me. I cannot create in chaos and this place is chaos."

He inhaled a steadying breath and held up both hands. "Dagmar, I emailed you yesterday telling you there was a delay receiving the tiles from Italy. I provided an alternate list of tasks to review today so we don't fall behind schedule. Did you read those?"

She pressed one long-taloned hand against her skin-tight zebra print blouse. "I am an artist. I create masterpieces. Without seeing the marble in person, I cannot be sure if my vision will come to fruition."

He glanced down at the plywood flooring and counted to five. "Look, I get it. But we have many other projects that need to be completed. We can work back in the restaurant or even go upstairs to the guest rooms."

Even though the guest rooms were slated for completion last but hey, this diva was a pain in the ass, and he just wanted her to do something. Anything but continue her tirade.

She jutted out one hip and flicked a hand, a stack of bracelets clanking. "Plans. Tasks. Do I look like I work off someone else's plans? You hired me to make this hotel unique and inviting. And I do things my way and I must have the tiles here first--"

"Look, we signed a contract, and we have deadlines. You're going to have to adapt and get your team started on something else first. Otherwise, we jeopardize our opening. I can review the spreadsheet I sent––" Heat crept up the back of his neck.

"You and your ridiculous spreadsheets. Don't you know who I am? The awards I've won? The elite hotels I've created? The celebrities who wouldn't dream of moving into their latest homes without me?" Her voice reached a pitch that likely only the pampered dogs in Beverly Hills could hear. They were probably streaming down Rodeo Drive in droves, like aliens returning to the Mother Ship.

Where was Jack or Austin when he needed them? They were "people persons" or whatever it was called. It wasn't as if he hadn't known there would be challenges transitioning from the behind the scenes finance guy to General Manager of Paramount. But the shit wasn't supposed to hit the fan already––not three months out from the New Year's Eve Grand Opening.

The situation was spiraling out of control. He'd spelled it out in black and white, for god's sake. He pushed his glasses up the bridge of his nose.

"Do you? Don't just stand there staring." She advanced closer on thigh-high white boots.

His jaw clicked shut and irritation flared up his spine. If only he was a magician and could make this banshee vanish in a poof of smoke. Or disappear down a trap-door.

An intoxicating citrusy scent filled the air and the hairs on the back of his neck prickled.

Brigitte stepped up and clasped Dagmar's hands. "Dagmar, *ma chérie*, there you are. Oh, you look even more fabulous than when I saw you for Paris fashion week. We're so honored to have you styling Paramount for us."

Like a switch flipping, the monster intent on assaulting

him flashed her fake white veneers. "Ah, Brigitte, you're here. Thank god, someone who understands."

Brigitte leaned in and kissed each of Dagmar's cheeks, French style. "Oh, have you been giving Lucas a tough time? You're so naughty. Tell me what's the matter on this perfect morning?"

Naughty? Seriously? Lucas's nostrils flared but he managed to keep his expression impassive. If Brigitte could get this woman in line, he'd roll with it. Hell, he'd be forever grateful.

Dagmar flapped her hands. "I was trying to tell *him* I simply cannot begin any work until the tiles arrive and they aren't here."

Brigitte turned, and the full force of her beauty slammed into him. Dark wavy hair framed a delicate, high-cheek boned face and her slate-blue eyes narrowed. "Oh, you must be having a misunderstanding. I'm sure we can figure everything out."

She pivoted back to Dagmar and continued in her husky accented voice. "Now, I know you've pulled off miracles. I mean, remember the work you did on that resort in the Maldives where half the materials arrived a month late and then half of them were cracked? You were the one written up in *Luxury World Travel* for saving the entire project."

Dagmar preened under Brigitte's sycophantic words. "Oh, I did do that, didn't I?"

Brigitte nodded, eyes sparkling, scarlet lips curved upwards. "You're the best. That's why we insisted nobody else would do for Paramount. And don't forget, the Hotel Kings chain is receiving tons of international attention. Once Paramount opens, we'll make sure you receive all the credit you deserve."

Lucas's internal eyeroll saved him from laughing out

loud. Somehow, Brigitte was handling this woman. Brigitte was not just beautiful; she was a miracle worker.

Dagmar pointed at him. "But he wants me to work off some plan? A checklist? Me? Can't you make him understand I don't work that way?"

Brigitte glanced at him and damn if she didn't wink. "Now Dagmar, Lucas is excellent at his job. And you always meet your deadlines, so you understand the pressure he's under as the G.M. I'm sure he didn't mean anything by it, did you, Lucas?"

His lips twitched. Oh, Brigitte was brilliant all right. And damn if she didn't have him under her spell, too. She'd even gotten him to kowtow to this woman. "Of course not. Opening Paramount on time is vital. I was just trying to help us work around the issue."

Was this what his new front office life was going to look like?

Brigitte placed one graceful hand on Dagmar's arm. "What if you and I look at the revised schedule together? This lobby will be child's play for you once the tiles arrive. Of course we can find somewhere else for you to work your magic. And won't it be more fun to start with a challenge? Maybe in the restaurant?"

Dagmar tossed her head again and glared at Lucas. "Maybe there are a few things we can do. But it is a huge sacrifice, you understand, don't you?"

"Of course. We all know how much sacrifice perfection takes. And this project will be nothing less than perfect. Now, let me chat with Lucas for a moment. Why don't you go down the street to Euro Caffe and order whatever you like, my treat. I'll meet you in a few minutes." Brigitte's voice was smooth as melted caramel.

"Okay. I've got some tear sheets in my portfolio. We can

review those. But under no circumstances will I work off spreadsheets." The designer shuddered.

She made working with a spreadsheet sound like shoveling manure, instead of the most practical invention of all time. But if she was going to stop yelling at him and do her damn job, he'd bite his tongue.

With a final sniff, she pivoted on her stilts and disappeared in a cloud of cloying rose perfume.

He massaged the tight cords on the back of his neck. If he survived until his hotel's opening day, it would be a fucking miracle. Dealing with budget issues and construction crews was one thing. Dagmar was something else.

"So I suppose I don't need to ask how you're doing today?" Brigitte's laugh was throaty.

A whole lot better since you arrived. He ran his tongue around his teeth. "It's fine. Hey, thank you for stepping in. Maybe you want to be that woman's handler? Because she is…a lot."

Her expression sobered. "Oh no, I will not. But don't worry, she's notoriously difficult to work with. Starting my first official day on-site with her means it's all downhill from here."

He shook his head. "I don't know how you do it but I'm glad you're here."

He worked to ignore the shiver racing down his spine. They hadn't spent much time alone. Not since they danced together at Ryan and Charlie's wedding. And the tightness in his chest was an untimely reminder that his crush on his concierge hadn't dissipated since Monterey. *Great.*

"Well, working as a concierge in 5 star hotels requires a little bit of finesse, especially dealing with the temperamental ones. You know here in Beverly Hills, people with dramatic personalities are more of the rule than the exception, right?" One groomed dark brow arched.

"So it seems. I'm hoping she's the toughest one—I'm not used to dealing with temper tantrums."

"Oh, she won't be the toughest, but she might be the loudest." Her smoky gaze raked him from head to toe. "And juggling all the personalities face-to-face is definitely different. But you've got the look, so that goes a long way."

"The look?" And damn if he didn't preen just like Dagmar. And fought to tamp down the flush rising in his cheeks. Being a ginger came with some bothersome physical traits.

She gave that sexy as hell laugh again. "Oh please, Lucas. It's pre-launch time with construction and dirt everywhere and you're in Tom Ford slacks and a white linen shirt. Do you even own jeans?"

"Hey, pot kettle black. What's your excuse?" He gestured at her silk shirt, gray pencil skirt, and sky-high stilettos.

Tried not to linger too long on her shapely legs.

Her lips twitched. "Touché. I have important meetings with potential clients today."

"I've got a few meetings today, too. And of course I wear jeans." So he liked nice clothes. Besides, he might dress like he was sophisticated, but she *was* sophisticated. She was from Paris, for god's sake.

She tapped one manicured finger against that tempting red mouth. "But now we're working together so I guess I'll see if you're always buttoned up."

Every muscle in his body hardened. Was she flirting with him? Because the phrase "buttoned up" immediately had his fingers flexing, imagining unfastening her violet blouse to discover if her creamy skin was as soft as it looked. How was he going to get over his infatuation with this woman now that he'd see her every day?

He forced a laugh. "Very funny. Anyway." *Compartmentalize, dude.*

Brigitte tilted her head, her gaze assessing. "Anyway? I'm going to meet with Dagmar. I'll get the situation sorted."

She gave him a mock salute, pivoted, and sauntered out the door. For a moment he simply stared. The woman's confidence, grace, and poise was something to behold.

"Great. Thanks. I'll be in my office if you need me." Relief coursed through him.

Because he couldn't afford any distractions, especially in the form of yearning for a woman who was out of his league. No matter how uncomfortable he was with stepping out of the background to center stage, he had made a commitment and he would never let down his friends and business partners.

Although today wasn't exactly an auspicious start.

Ryan, who had the bulk of the hotel experience, ran Pacific Jewel Inn in La Jolla. Jack transitioned from the lead attorney to head up Maison du Soleil in Paso Robles, Cameron went from a military captain to lead Cypress Coast Ranch in Monterey, and Austin gave up his career as a rock-star to be head of The Monroe in Palm Springs.

Now it was his turn to step up to the plate and no way in hell would he be the weak link and let his band of brothers down. And he wouldn't fall for Brigitte the way his buddies had each fallen for one of their co-workers.

Although working closely with Brigitte Thibault during pre-launch would present some challenges, he needed her to help him navigate business situations, not personal ones. And even if the vibrant, easy-going woman would be attracted to someone as tightly wound and nerdy as him, he wasn't the kind of guy who could handle a fling.

He headed down the wide, high-ceilinged hallway to his office. The hotel buzzed with activity, hammers and drills and sounds of change. None of the construction crew had problems working from task lists. And so far, nobody had pitched a fit when asked to switch gears.

He crossed the large room and sank into his chair behind his enormous teak desk and powered up his computer. Time to focus on what he loved to do--control the numbers.

CHAPTER 2

*B*rigitte smiled up at the towering palm trees and savored the crisp breeze as she crossed Dayton Way after her meeting with Dagmar. The perpetual sunshine, bursts of brilliant bougainvillea, and immaculate shops and cafés suited her.

So far, Beverly Hills was living up to her expectations, especially the over-the-top personalities. Recalling how the tips of Lucas's ears glowed red as he faced off with Dagmar deepened her smile––she'd enjoyed saving the day. Over a double espresso, she'd redirected Dagmar to some other projects to keep the renovation on track. Crisis averted.

Time to return to her office and prepare for her own appointment. She'd almost reached the entrance when her phone rang with an unknown number.

"May I please speak with Brigitte Thibault?" An unfamiliar voice asked.

"This is Brigitte. What can I do for you?" With the new job and the new town, every call could potentially be hotel business.

"Hi Brigitte, my name is Tracee Leduq and I'm a recruiter based in New York. I've got an exceptional offer for you."

Curiosity flickered through her, but she squashed it. Hadn't she been feeling content? "Thank you for thinking of me. But I've just started a new position in Beverly Hills."

"I do know you've recently started at Paramount, but my client asked specifically for you. This is a unique opportunity for the right person. Will you at least let me tell you about it?"

She nibbled on her lower lip. Hearing about the position didn't mean she was being disloyal, did it? "Well, I am committed to my role here but okay, I'll listen."

"Excellent. My client owns numerous luxury properties around the world. He's seeking someone who can go to one locale, get the concierge service programs up and running and then move to the next resort. Each assignment would last roughly six months to one year. We know your track record of working all over the world, and it seems you prefer variety so this could be a perfect fit?"

"How do you know so much about my career?" And how did they know this position was her ultimate dream job? Where had this type of position been before she'd decided to try out California?

The woman cleared her throat. "The luxury hospitality world is tiny, as you know. You've got an outstanding reputation and you've never made it a secret you enjoy shorter assignments."

"Thank you again but again, I'm not looking to move right now." But she couldn't deny the flutter of excitement in her belly. And the matching twinge of regret.

Tracee pounced. "Well, my client is flexible and can afford to wait. How long is your assignment there in Beverly Hills?"

She pressed one hand to her now uneasy belly. Damn it.

She'd accepted the position at Paramount because she wanted to work with her best friend again. After living all over the globe, she'd craved somewhere new. And Charlie Ray was her only family––not just her best friend but more of a sister. Or at least what she imagined it would feel like to have a sister.

Over the close to two years since Charlie started as V.P. of Sales and Marketing, Brigitte had been ready to join the close-knit Hotel Kings group. The guys were more like brothers than corporate colleagues––a family, not just a business. She'd promised Charlie she'd stay at Paramount after opening, at least for a while. And it would be unfair to leave Lucas to handle all the Dagmars and challenges during pre-launch.

"Are you still on the line? If you're curious, the compensation package is top of the line."

When the recruiter tossed out an exorbitant figure, she gasped. "What's the catch? Who is your client?"

It was more than double what she was making now––too good to be true.

"No catch, just another level of exclusivity and the owner is willing to compensate for the best. And I'm sure you're aware I'm not at liberty to disclose my client's information unless we move forward with the interview process."

"Oh, of course. Well, thank you for thinking of me but I've committed to this position." So why did that familiar tingle of longing for something new have to appear?

"Of course, I understand but please think about it. May I reach out to you again in a few months just in case circumstances change?"

Keeping her options open had always worked for her in the past. Although she had no intention of leaving, she'd always started out in each new job, each new town, hell, each new country, with the hope it would finally feel like home.

In the end she was always ready to move on. But now she'd be working with her best friend and live close to her again, which she anticipated making all the difference. But leaving her options open wouldn't hurt anything.

"Okay. But I am committed to Paramount, just so you know." Was she trying to convince the recruiter or herself?

Because maybe Beverly Hills could be long-term. The fancy little town was small enough to have its own personali-ty--which the jury was still out on--yet large enough not to feel isolated. Just because she thought she'd feel more connection to her new home immediately didn't mean she wouldn't soon.

More importantly, she owed it to herself, her best friend, and the Hotel Kings to stay the course. She would give one hundred percent. At least until the hotel launched success-fully. By then, she'd have a better idea if this place was a fit. Resolute, she dropped her phone into her purse and strode back to the hotel, her heels clicking on the pristine sidewalk and the sun warming her back.

BRIGITTE CROSSED through Paramount's majestic entrance, well what would be the entrance once the signage and new front doors were installed, and retreated to her small office. She closed the door, sagged back against the firm wood, and allowed her eyes to flutter closed. What a morning.

She settled onto her swivel-chair and sifted through the clutter on her sleek desk. Everything from coffee table books, local culture guides, and celebrity biographies crowded the surface. Between appointments, she was immersing herself in everything local. Where was the Teuscher Chocolates pamphlet? She had a meeting to discuss an exclusive deal for the hotel in an hour.

With a triumphant exclamation, she located it underneath one of a few unopened cardboard boxes. She smoothed the crumpled paper for one more thorough review. Charlie teased her for being messy, but her system of organization worked for her. Admittedly one nobody else had ever decoded but that wasn't her concern.

If Lucas came in, he'd likely break out in hives. From what she'd seen, the man's office was pristine without a stray file or extraneous scrap of paper anywhere. But it wasn't totally spartan––he had a few fantastic photos, including one from the Pacific Jewel Inn, the chain's flagship hotel, at its opening gala, which she'd attended.

The only personal item in her office was her favorite coffee mug which proclaimed, *"We'll be the old ladies causing trouble in the nursing homes,"* which Charlie had given her back in their Miami days. Not that she felt the need to personalize the space because as concierge she was out and about most of the day. So this room was strictly for behind the scenes and a place to stash a spare pair of Louboutins.

She spun in her chair, gazed out the picture window at the postcard view, and checked her phone. Three messages and two missed calls from Charlie. Uh-oh, her best friend had a sixth sense, did she know she'd been talking to someone about another job already?

She hit FaceTime. *"Bonjour,* Charlie. Everything okay?"

Her best friend's enormous onyx eyes were wide. "Tell me you made it to Paramount ahead of Dagmar?"

"Not exactly ahead of her but I arrived on time. Why?" *Oui,* Charlie was psychic.

"Oh good. Well, I wanted to talk to you about Lucas. And then I saw Dagmar on the schedule, and I panicked because I wanted you there as a buffer."

"Why did you panic? I mean, besides the obvious with her?"

"Well, maybe I'm overreacting. I meant to bring this up earlier, but things have been so hectic with the opening of The Monroe in Palm Springs and prepping for Paramount."

Charlie's voice lowered dramatically. Which, with her theatrical friend, was not unusual. "So, I've got a little favor to ask you."

"Of course. What do you need?"

"Okay, I was hoping you could help out Lucas over the next few months until Jon and Dave Golden get on-site. We need someone more extroverted to balance out Lucas because he's shy, bordering on socially anxious with people he doesn't know, even though he's handsome and a dead ringer for Jamie in *Outlander*."

"Balance him out? He seems perfectly capable to me." And, yes, she'd noticed he was quite handsome with his strong square jaw, chiseled cheekbones, and surprisingly sensual mouth for a man so focused on boring numbers. She'd be blind if she failed to notice how he was built like a Scottish highlander, at least the ones she'd seen on television.

Although Dagmar had thrown him for a loop.

"He's a genius with numbers and has been our backbone for all the financing and budgets for the hotels. He absolutely has the business skills to step into the G.M. role, but now he has to schmooze and be charming with guests, employees, city officials of our fanciest hotel. While you're always charming."

She smirked at Charlie. "Ooh, la la. *Merci*, you think I'm charming and fancy?"

Charlie snorted. "Oh please, Ms. Fancypants. You were too big for the Turks and Caicos, and no other location in California would do for you. But it's more about handling the difficult people, like Dagmar, and the clientele Paramount will attract."

She shrugged. "But that's what's entertaining about it.

Exceeding those people's lofty expectations is what it's all about. And that's what we shall do here."

"And that's why you're the perfect person for the job. And if you can help Lucas see how you juggle twenty things at once and never have a hair out of place, that would go a long way because he's a little rigid."

She cleared her throat. "Well, I have a lot on my plate already. Can't Ryan help, and isn't the new Sales and Marketing guy going to be here soon?"

Because she'd finally escaped the sheer boredom of living on a small resort island and babysitting a 36-year-old man wasn't exactly appealing. Not that she would ever take the time to babysit any man. Or woman for that matter. Never had. Never would.

Charlie's dark brows drew together. "Well, you're the most perfect, and most talented, person to do it. And you know I'm a control freak and I want Paramount to be a huge success. Pretty please?"

A laugh bubbled up her throat. "Because you're not, how you Americans say, "buttering my cookie" to get me to do what you want?"

Charlie giggled. "It's butter your muffin. Not cookie. And you know I think you should be running that hotel or at least have taken the Assistant G.M. role."

"You know that's not for me. Anyway, what are you suggesting? Because you know I'll be going out to a lot of appointments, and I cannot sacrifice that." Establishing the relationships in Beverly Hills was key to keeping the guests happy when they weren't at the hotel.

"A few things off the top of my head: there's an issue with the outdoor dining permit, three head chefs have already bitten the dust, and I'm concerned that the next one will be a prima donna, too. And of course, keeping Dagmar on deadline."

Brigitte sniffed. "So, if I help with these tasks, that's it?"

The sooner the hotel was running smoothly, the more confident Lucas would feel running it. And whether she stayed or left Beverly Hills wouldn't impact the Hotel Kings. Not that she was planning on leaving or taking the dream job offer, but no need to make herself indispensable.

"Okay, I'll do what I can, but I need to focus on my job, too." Actually, maybe she would enjoy helping Lucas. He was sweet, even if he was a little stuffy.

"Well, don't forget, the guys and yours truly are coming up in two weeks to sit down and review the 30-60-90 day plan to opening day. Kenzie's going to come up from Palm Springs for the spa manager interviews, but I don't think Lucy or Campbell can make it."

"That's too bad, it could have been a full party. I made reservations for everyone at that new Escape Room out in the Valley, so that should be a fun way to blow off steam after the serious stuff, right?"

Charlie barked out a laugh. "I never thought I'd see the day my Parisian friend thought going to an Escape Room would be fun. Look how far you've come now you're back in the U.S."

Brigitte rolled her eyes. "Oh, please. We went to one in London, if you recall. And I wasn't the only one having fun."

A voice sounded in the background and Charlie turned and called something over her shoulder. "Sorry about that. Ryan's here. I'll see you soon but keep me posted on how everything's going. Love you, bye." And the screen went dark.

A sense of bemusement filled Brigitte. The way her best friend's expression softened when she mentioned her new husband's name still surprised her. Not that she wasn't thrilled for the love they had found together but back in the day, Ryan and Charlie had been archenemies. Now they were married.

She and Charlie had never had close long-term relationships for a host of reasons. They had both had isolated childhoods and bonded over that abandoned little girl they'd both buried deep beneath their polished exteriors. So when Charlie tumbled head over heels with Ryan...it was a shock.

It made her happy to see Charlie so happy, but she still didn't quite understand it. Of course, she'd cared about some of the men she'd been involved with, but she'd never experienced whatever connection Charlie and Ryan shared.

Granted, part of her single status was the hospitality industry. And perhaps a bigger part was her choice not to allow anyone too close. Charlie was the first person she'd let in.

For years, it had been Charlie and Brigitte, Brigitte and Charlie, kind of like Thelma and Louise. And now everything had changed. Not that Charlie wasn't fully present for her but now Ryan was Charlie's ride or die. Somehow, she'd thought they would spend more time together once she'd arrived in California.

Her throat tightened but she swallowed down the unfamiliar pang of emotion. She tucked away the thoughts of love and marriage and switched back to her default comfort zone--work.

She loved her role as concierge--bringing people together with the best experiences for them so they fell in love with not only the hotel but the location. She prided herself on finding the perfect activity or café for the perfect person at the perfect time. Of course, that included keeping whatever services she could in-house but developing strong relationships with all the locals was vital to establishing the hotel as a long-term fixture in the fickle neighborhood. She relished the challenge.

Of course, she was happy to help Lucas with some of the

stickier situations, of which she was sure there would be many. And maybe it would be a fun challenge?

She checked her watch--time to go to her own appointment and focus on Beverly Hills.

CHAPTER 3

"Yes, it's all handled. You know you don't have to check in with me every day. I've got everything under control." More like, he had everything under control now that Brigitte had saved his ass. But no need for Ryan to know about that.

Ryan blew out an exasperated exhale. "Dude, we all helped with every single hotel launch, remember? So you're really going to piss me off if you don't keep me in the loop. I mean, I know we handled the permits before renovations started but Beverly Hills has some additional local requirements that can be a pain in the ass."

His best friend and boss was not only the CEO, Ryan was also a complete control freak. And everyone gave *him* crap about being uptight.

"I know, I'm meeting with the guy from Fast Facilitator Permits for dinner tonight. He's supposed to ensure we didn't miss anything with the outdoor dining permit for Belcanto since we decided on that after other approvals. You're in the loop as much as you need to be."

"Okay, okay."

"And we'll all be together in a few weeks, and we'll go through every single permit, contract, and plan in more detail than you've ever wanted. I've got a spreadsheet with all the problems, don't worry. I'm not going to call you ten times a day with trivial questions. I've got it figured out."

"Like Austin had you helping him behind the scenes with the numbers he had figured out in Palm Springs?" Ryan's smirk traveled through the phone.

"Or how you've had to learn to live with Charlie always being right?" His alpha buddy had met his match when Charlie Ray had blown into town like a tsunami.

"Funny. So, how is it going with Brigitte?"

"What do you mean, how's it going?" *Shit*. He rolled his shoulders and strode across his office to the wide picture window. The last thing he needed was for Ryan or any of his friends to find out he had a crush on Brigitte.

"I just meant how is it working with her? Is she doing a good job?"

He studied the view of N. Canon Avenue. Admired the meticulously maintained white flowers, endless palm trees, and an eclectic mix of architecture, while he ensured his voice stayed neutral. "Brigitte's much better with people than I am.. Are you sure you don't want to have me to stay on as CFO instead?"

Ryan pounced. "You're going to do great. And she's incredible with the public. It's just you're used to running the show behind the curtain, like the Wizard of Oz. All I'm saying is I'm on speed dial, okay?"

He chuckled and shook his head. "The Wizard of Oz? Seriously, man?"

Ryan barked out a laugh. "Good one, right? Look, you and I are alike--we get shit done behind the scenes. And if I can pull off being welcoming to guests, so can you. Not everyone can charm the world like Jack does or hell, scare them into submission like Cam."

Yeah, their two friends were different and impactful in their own way. "Fair point. Got it. Look, I've got back to back meetings the rest of the morning. I'll catch you later."

"Remember. Call me anytime and I'll see you in a few weeks. Later."

No, I'm not calling—I'll figure this shit out myself. Yeah, he was being stubborn, but he needed to do this on his own. At least as well as the rest of the guys had. He couldn't let them down—meeting them in college had changed his life. They were the first people who made him feel like he belonged.

Although the six-week hotel training Ryan had given them was almost two years ago, he'd played a part in opening each of the first four hotels and had learned along the way.

He'd already hired several people. Interviews were straightforward because he could read resumés and control the environment. Besides, Dave Golden would be arriving soon to run Sales and Marketing, and Jon would move up to Beverly Hills in December to be his Assistant General Manager.

The property was buzzing with activity in preparation for their on-time and on-budget opening day. And as it was planning time, he strode to his desk and flipped open his laptop. A host of various subcontractors were hammering away in their respective sections of the hotel. The lead contractor, Travis, was organized and responsible. No need to worry about him or his crew.

Everything was on track.

"Knock, knock." Brigitte stood framed in the doorway, her sharp cheekbones flushed and her tip-tilted eyes gleaming.

He cleared his throat. "Hi. Thanks again for this morning." And why did his gut tighten the moment he saw her?

"Like I said, it's nothing. I can handle people like Dagmar in my sleep. It's my superpower. I wanted to check and see if we could do a quick walk-through because I have a few logistical questions?" She sauntered into the office and suddenly the large space shrank. Her visceral presence filled the room.

"Of course." He checked his chrome diver's watch. "I don't have another appointment until after lunch. Does that work?" Later this afternoon, he was meeting an administrator in the Police Department for valet parking permits, which were imperative for check-in and diners coming to the restaurant, Belcanto. The parking garage for the building was small and street parking was practically non-existent.

"*Oui*, that would be perfect."

"Let's do it." He rose from the chair. They were co-workers, their best friends were married to each other, they were all part of one big happy work family. So why did he hesitate to step out from behind the desk?

Her scarlet lips curved upward, revealing even white teeth. "I appreciate it. This is the first time I've been on board during pre-launch, so I don't want to miss anything. We need to make Ryan and Charlie proud, right?"

His jaw tightened. "I just got off the phone with him."

She tucked a strand of dark hair behind her ear and looked up at him. "He and Charlie are like Mother Hens. I believe I received the "we're all a family here and you can reach out 24/7" speech a hundred times since I accepted the role."

His lips twitched. "Ryan was our platoon leader in ROTC and in his mind, he always will be. Anyway, how are you liking L.A. so far?" Keep the conversation friendly. Professional.

"It's not Paris or New York but it beats living on that little island. Don't get me wrong, it was beautiful there but so small. I prefer having the buzz of a city around me."

"Same." Huh, something they had in common. After growing up in a small agricultural town, he thrived on the energy of a city. Beverly Hills itself was tiny, but Los Angeles boasted excellent restaurants, all the entertainment you could want, and the perfect weather in Southern California enabled him to be outside year-round.

They crossed the plywood covered floors toward the lobby in companionable silence. She was an extroverted, talkative woman but apparently she had no desire to fill the air with chatter. It was refreshing.

The tension around the base of his skull softened and he gazed around the lobby with appreciation. They'd been fortunate the existing structure boasted high ceilings and large rectangular shaped windows, allowing natural light to stream into the space. Once the drywall was complete, the walls would be subtle alabaster-white, and they'd installed delicate crown molding to add more European flair to the seven story, twenty-five room hotel.

A few columns broke up the space and custom velvet couches would encircle the marble. They'd taken Dagmar the Dragon's advice to upholster them in a Tiffany-box-blue. A popular color in Southern California.

Once the damn custom black and white tiles arrived, they would be set on the diagonal, like some of the gorgeous lobbies in France's swankiest hotels. If all went according to plan, Paramount would feel like you'd stepped into a hotel in any of Europe's most sophisticated cities.

"So hit me with your questions." Because it would be nice to be the one with the answers.

Brigitte stopped in front of the built-in antique mahogany table that would serve as the reception desk and ran her fingers along the unique piece. "I have a few questions but oh, they did such a beautiful job with the reception desk. It's a work of art."

He smiled in satisfaction. "And it's efficient. It's in the perfect spot to keep an eye on the front door and large enough for two people behind it without being crowded."

Her laugh was throaty. "Of course, the efficiency is what you see."

"What's wrong with efficiency?" And damn it, the back of his neck warmed from the teasing note in her voice.

"Nothing at all. But I did have another question about all of you being in the ROT together? We don't have this in France and Charlie tried to explain it to me but I'm not sure I understand. You were all in the military after university?"

"ROTC. It's a scholarship program where the military pays for your college education in exchange for either serving active duty or joining the reserves. Cam is the only one who served and the rest of us were in the reserves."

Her eyes widened. "That is a good program. But you had uniforms and training, yes?"

"We did. We had to train for a month in the summers and that's probably why we all grew so close. The guys are my brothers in everything but blood." They were his family.

She nodded. "Like Charlie and me. I understand. How did you go from that to luxury hotels?"

"So we were in the Army program and one summer, they had us camping out in the middle of nowhere and it was hell sleeping on the ground. We came up with the plan to open luxury hotels one day because we never wanted to sleep on a pile of rocks again."

She threw back her head and laughed. "That's fantastic. A bunch of college boys hatching a plan. And you brought it to fruition. It's incredible what you've created. And it makes sense--Ryan is the one who went straight into hospitality, and you all built other skills to contribute. Brilliant."

He stood a little taller at her praise. "Charlie said you're the best and after this morning, I don't doubt her."

She slipped him a curious glance. "Oh, you had doubts?"

"Of course not. No, no doubts." And he was about to stammer again. Her confidence was compelling. Brigitte scrambled his brain. Not to mention heated his blood.

"Hmmph, I would hope not. Now I wanted to discuss the cigar lounge with you. How is it coming along?" She crossed the hall and paused in front of a set of double doors.

Discussing the exclusive salon was something he could focus on instead of her. They stepped into a boxy windowless space, and now the scent of her exotic perfume filled his senses. He strode to the far wall, which would be built-in floor to ceiling glass cabinets designed to display some of the cigar boxes and a few choice bottles of Macallan and other top-shelf whiskies.

"Fantastic actually. These plans are approved so we don't need to consult with Diva—I mean Dagmar. The drywall will be hung by the end of the week, then the glass installed, and finally the floors. Did you see the photos yet?"

He could picture it now––the walls a deep rich cabernet paired with honey-oak plank floors. Low-slung tobacco-brown leather couches, espresso-colored deep armchairs, a few low tables, and library style lamps. Austin, who had overseen the food and beverage set up for all the hotels, had chosen the colors to complement the whiskey, wine, and cigars.

She spun in a slow pirouette, graceful as a ballerina. "I love it. I did see the photos and it has such a warm, masculine feel. But I'm still concerned about the cigar smoke. You Americans are much more sensitive, especially here in California."

He retreated a step, pushed his glasses up the bridge of his nose. "That's the cool thing. The architect figured out a way to seal the two sets of doors, which will be an opaque etched glass. When they're closed, not a whiff of smoke can escape. Even if a whisper got through the first door, and into the mudroom/snug area, the seal around the lobby door is practically impenetrable. It's magic."

"Oh, *c'est super* and will feel very private and exclusive." She clapped her hands together. "I love it. I feel like this would be an excellent place for me to reserve for guests who are handling low-key business and want a more intimate setting."

He nodded. "Exactly. Deals over cigars instead of conference tables. Did you have any more questions about the space?" Because his heart was beating too fast and he needed a little distance.

"You answered without me having to ask. You are very efficient." She winked.

Again, a flush crept up the back of his neck. Yeah, being in close proximity with Brigitte messed with his equilibrium. There was something about her confidence that was incredibly attractive. Not to mention she smelled like heaven, and he was in danger of leaning over to sniff her.

He forced himself to focus––he was a 36-year-old man for god's sake, not the awkward teenager from his past. "It's my superpower. Let's check on the spa next because the tile setters are there."

"Perfect. And I'm sure Kenzie's input will make it as incredible as The Monroe's spa. I want to ensure our guests stay here and don't check out the others around town."

His phone buzzed––Donnie Filipovich from Fast Facilitator confirming a business dinner he'd been dreading for weeks.

"Everything okay?" Brigitte placed one graceful hand on his forearm and he hissed out a breath.

"Just confirmation for a business dinner I'd rather not

attend. This guy runs a company that expedites necessary permits. Beverly Hills has a lot of rules, and we missed the deadline for an outdoor dining permit."

"Can I help?"

He ran his tongue around his teeth and figured *fuck it.* "You don't have plans?"

The corners of her eyes crinkled. "*Non.* You're the only person I know in town."

"You know Dagmar."

She rolled her eyes. "Oh please, as if I'd voluntarily spend time with her."

"Maybe you could come and help me get him talking? He's supposed to help us navigate with the council and he's been tough to pin down. I know you're busy but…"

"But I need to eat?" She smiled sweetly.

"Exactly. And you're charming. You've got a knack with people." *Which I don't have and likely never will.*

Her lips twitched. "You mean dealing with tantrums from strangers?"

"Basically. I know this guy likes his wine and can ramble but a dinner at The Penthouse at Mastro's can't be too bad, right?"

"I am happy to help where I can. And I enjoyed the Mastro's in Palm Springs. And if my boss believes his concierge should eat there before recommending it to our guests, who am I to say no? What time?" She grinned mischievously.

He returned her playful smile. "8 p.m."

"I've got to run. I will meet you there at 8."

"That would be great. Thanks." He'd be able to hit the boxing gym and get in a few rounds with the punching bag. Because being around Brigitte had his adrenaline pumping and he needed to channel it somewhere.

"*Merci.* I'll see you later, Lucas." She pivoted and crossed the high-ceilinged space toward the offices on the other side of reception.

He exhaled a steadying breath and tucked away Ms. Brigitte Thibault in the vault. He had a feeling it wouldn't be the last time.

CHAPTER 4

*L*ucas tapped his foot as he waited by the hostess stand at Mastro's Steakhouse. He'd arrived fifteen minutes early because he'd wanted to beat Filipovich. The lobby hummed with activity, animated conversations, and background music.

From prior experience, he knew this was one of those restaurants where people went to be seen. And from what he'd learned from researching Filipovich, that's exactly what the guy wanted. Especially because the Penthouse had a louder, more social vibe than the classic steakhouse downstairs he frequented for business dinners. He dreaded the hectic scene, but he needed this guy's help.

When he glanced at the entrance, his breath lodged in his throat. A brunette goddess sauntered in through the glass doors. Every person in the place turned and stared--her presence was that captivating--even in the celebrity filled town.

And had all the noise dissipated? He blinked twice and focused in on Brigitte. She'd looked beautiful today in her professional clothes but tonight? *Damn.*

Sky-high sandals emphasized her long, shapely legs and the red wrap dress matched her lips perfectly. She looked elegant, yet incredibly sexy and she exuded confidence as she crossed the lobby to join him. He ground his molars together to ensure his jaw didn't drop to the floor. The woman embodied every fantasy wrapped up into one striking package.

She joined him, a smile lighting up her oval face. "You weren't joking when you said this place is quite the scene."

Her exotic scent enveloped him, and he managed to answer with what he hoped was his normal voice. "I was not. And apparently the Penthouse has even more of a party vibe. We'll see."

She surveyed the space, her eyes speculative. "Everyone here looks air brushed. Not sure how you Americans maintain the flawlessness."

As if she wasn't the most flawless one. "Well, Beverly Hills is the plastic surgery capital and celebrities have to keep up."

She winked. "Well, then I'm glad we aren't celebrities."

He shuddered. "Yeah, living in the spotlight isn't for me. But it's entertaining to observe, and we'll see a lot of it here. You okay with that?"

"Of course." She shrugged. "It's all part of the luxury hotel world but it's a little extra here."

Lucas's phone buzzed and he glanced down. "Excuse me, it's Filipovich, and he's canceling last minute." What a douche.

"Seriously? This late?" She wrinkled her small, straight nose.

He gave a curt nod. "Seriously."

The hostess approached, "Sutton, party of three for The Penthouse. Are you all here?"

"No, now we're just two." He turned to Brigitte. "Is that okay with you?" Which meant they were practically on a date together. Sweat prickled between his shoulder blades—it was one thing hiding his crush at work, but at a table for two?

She shrugged a shoulder. "We're here. Of course."

They followed the hostess past the shaker stone columns, floor-to-ceiling wine cabinets, and terracotta colored ceilings to the staircase. Glittering modern chandeliers and tan marble-looking walls gave the restaurant a warm, welcoming feel.

Once they were seated, Brigitte perused the wine menu and he studied his menu, working to play it cool. This was a work dinner, not a romantic date, despite the white-table-clothed table.

"I hope you'll allow me to order the wine—it's one of my passions. But shall we start with whiskey? I'm assuming we're having steak?"

It would take a barrel of whiskey to quiet his racing pulse every time he was near her. "Absolutely on the whiskey and the wine. And yes on the steak—it's what they're known for, but the seafood is excellent, too."

When the waitress returned, Lucas ordered them two glasses of Midelton Very Rare, neat. He remembered Brigitte's moan of pleasure when she'd sampled a fine Irish whiskey at Ryan and Charlie's recent wedding in Monterey. And he remembered how she'd felt in his arms when they'd danced. How he'd almost kissed her. How he'd felt like he'd been struck by lightning, but she'd flitted away, as if he'd been the only one impacted.

"So do we really need to work with this guy or are there alternatives to expedite the permit?"

He sipped his drink, allowing the smooth flavor to wash over his palate. "In an ideal world, yes, he's the one but he does have a few partners. Restaurants are his specialty, though. And who knows, maybe he did have an emergency."

"You're very generous. Well, he's rude to cancel at the time of the reservation. Quite the way to send a message. So you'll work around him?" She raised a brow.

He laughed. "Exactly. At least we can enjoy dinner. Sorry I dragged you out so late."

"It's not too late for dinner. I'm French, remember? I don't know if I'll ever grow accustomed to how early people eat here. Let's enjoy the meal so I can give a genuine recommendation to our guests." Brigitte laughed.

"Yes." Although how was he going to make it through dinner when the throaty sound shot sparks of heat along his skin and the golden lighting highlighted how fucking beautiful she was?

"Mmm-hmm. A Rhone blend should be perfect with the filet and the garlic mashed potatoes. I love a good cut of red meat." She snapped the menu shut and placed it on the polished wood table.

He stiffened. What the hell was wrong with him? How could her saying she liked red meat turn him on? He needed to pull himself together. Brigitte's presence was intoxicating, and he needed to remember his priorities.

Make that priority, singular. Paramount. That was his only priority for the foreseeable future. Period.

Fortunately, the server appeared and took their orders. Lucas exhaled a steadying breath, and they sat back and finished their whiskies in companionable silence. The piano music filled the space, and the dynamic atmosphere was helping him forget the long day.

The waitress appeared and uncorked the bottle of French red. Brigitte swirled the wine, inhaled, and moaned. Once again, every muscle leapt to attention, and he adjusted in his seat. Damn, was everything the woman did some kind of over-the-top sensual experience?

"Good?" Yeah, his voice was a little squeaky.

"It's excellent. Dense, bold, with hints of lavender and dark fruit. Quite a mouthful. It will be perfect with the filet." Her eyes gleamed in the restaurants gilded lighting.

Time to change the subject to anything other than her mouth. "Hey, so tell me how you got so good handling people like Dagmar? Share your tricks." Because odds were he'd need to ask her for help again. Better her than one of the guys.

"Well, I think part of it is I've moved around a lot my whole life. Charlie said I was like one of those, what do you call them, military imps?"

His lips twitched. "I think you mean military brats. Were your parents in the military?" Shouldn't he have known this about her? Especially since Cam had served for more than a decade, and Jack actually was a military brat.

She shrugged and winked. "Imps, brats––not so different. No, my parents weren't in the military, but my *Maman* didn't like staying in one place too long. So, let's just say I was at a new school most years. You learn to read people really quickly."

What she didn't say hit him hard. He'd been lucky to have two stable parents and grow up in the same house. Although, being one of the biggest nerds in a small town wasn't exactly ideal, either. Before his growth spurt in eleventh grade, he would have given anything to move to a new town. He shook his head––no need to go back there.

"I bet. Jack's easy with people, the way you are. So, what's the longest you've stayed in one spot?"

Her gaze lifted over his shoulder, seemingly studying the floor-to-ceiling wall of wine behind him. "Hmm, I lasted at Cerulean Eden for almost five years."

"And you were ready to go, I take it?"

She slid him a guarded look. "I was bored out of my mind

after Charlie left. It was an excellent experience, but I was eager to leave."

"Well, their loss is our gain." Keep it about work and don't start wondering about her childhood. "And if you handle difficult people like you did this morning, we're probably not paying you enough."

She pursed her lips. "Ooh, do I get a raise already? I like it."

He swallowed a groan––that mouth. He adjusted in his seat and salvation appeared in the form of a waiter with two steaming cups of lobster bisque.

Brigitte sniffed the fragrant dish and moaned again. Holy shit, this woman was going to kill him with these sensual noises. He'd better focus on his soup, or he'd never survive until dessert.

They made it through the first course and the wine softened his nerves. He was a successful businessman and not the geeky kid he'd been. Not anymore. He could handle one self-assured brilliant woman. Even one who had dominated his thoughts way too often since that dance in Monterey.

The waitress had just cleared their plates when a cheesy looking blond guy materialized next to Brigitte. Maybe he was the maître d or even the sommelier? But, no, because they were smack in the middle of Beverly Hills and The Penthouse, it couldn't be that straightforward.

"Hello there, doll," the man addressed Brigitte and totally ignored him. "Has anyone told you that you could be Marion Cotillard's twin sister? Are you?" His voice oozed smarm.

Annoyance flickered down Lucas's spine and he set down his wineglass. Was this guy for real? Before he could open his mouth, Brigitte gave the guy a once over.

She tapped her index finger against her scarlet lips and shook her head. "I was told that in Los Angeles people were discreet. And you come to our dinner table with this?"

Her disdain flew right over the guy's oiled hair. "I knew you were French. Sorry beautiful, but I'm a big-time movie producer. With your looks and my connections, I can make you a star. I can't take the chance of someone else snapping you up first."

Lucas leaned back in his chair, crossed his arms, and waited for the show. No need for him to step up and protect Brigitte––the woman could handle anyone.

She picked up her wineglass, took a sip, and set the glass on the table before deigning to respond. The man stood there, a smirk on his face, likely assuming she was trying to gather her composure before leaping for joy.

She raked her gaze from the top of the "movie producer's" head to his slip-on Italian loafers. "First of all, I'm aware that everyone in this town thinks they are a movie producer. I, however, am not an actress nor do I have any desire to be one.

"And if I were, I certainly wouldn't entertain offers from a person rude enough to interrupt me during a meal. Now, please go away." She shooed him away with one hand and turned back to Lucas.

The jerk's face suffused with red, and his eyebrows would have drawn together if his face lift hadn't pulled his skin so tight. "No need to be a little bitch. And now I've seen you up close, you're too old to make it here anyway."

Brigitte ignored him and picked up her wineglass.

Lucas's rose to his feet, and his hands curled into fists. This asshole wasn't going to disrespect Brigitte. "I suggest you get out of here right now or I'll remove you myself."

"Lucas." Brigitte's voice was husky.

"I said now." He took two steps toward the guy, who immediately jumped back.

"I don't need to waste my time here." With a curl of his lip, the "producer" scuttled away.

Once he ensured the guy was descending the stairs, Lucas sank back into his seat. He took a steadying breath before looking at Brigitte. What was this stab of protectiveness?

She considered him, a gleam in her smoky eyes. "You know, there was no need for you to defend me. That little man wasn't worth it."

He shrugged. "I know you had him handled but I will not sit by while someone speaks to you that way." Call him old-fashioned, but his mother had taught him to be a gentleman.

And he'd learned at a young age that nasty people tended to scurry off the moment someone called their bluff. Like that loser.

After a moment, her lips curved up. "*Merci.* I'm not used to people defending me, but he was a rude little creature, wasn't he?"

"He was." Warmth filled his chest. If she wasn't used to someone having her back, he was happy to stand in.

The server appeared with their filets and sides of garlic mashed potatoes and asparagus. The ugly scene forgotten, they savored the meal together. Which was welcome after the drama of the day. After dinner, they stepped outside just as Brigitte's rideshare pulled up to the curb.

"You're sure you don't want a ride?"

They lived on the same block in Brentwood, which hadn't struck him as dangerous before today. But with each moment he spent with her, he fell a little deeper under her spell. Not that she had a clue. No more fancy dinners alone together.

"No, I've got to finish a few things at the office. But thanks again for a great day." Time to create and maintain a professional distance between them.

"Thank you for dinner and for defending my honor." She placed one hand lightly on his chest and kissed him on one cheek and then the other, like she had in Monterey.

The hint of wine and chocolate mousse, her exotic citrusy scent, and the brush of her red lips on his skin almost undid him. He managed to maintain his composure and waved a hand, like he hadn't almost turned his head and captured her tempting mouth with his.

He was in so much trouble.

CHAPTER 5

$\mathcal{B}$rigitte drummed her fingers on the one clear spot on her desk and texted Lucas again. It was unlike him not to answer straight away, and it was imperative she speak with him now. Because she had a deal that could elevate their status in the Beverly Hills uber-competitive luxury hotel business, and she had to give verbal approval tonight. The clock was ticking.

She blew out an impatient breath. Where was he?

Aha, she could check on the master calendar schedule because the man lived by a time clock. Not that she was a habitually late person but if the man said five on the dot, he meant five on the dot.

And it was now 5:15. She pulled up the calendar and he'd marked himself out for the evening, which was unusual. Not that she was paying that close of attention or anything.

In fact, since the dinner at Mastro's, she'd barely seen him––a glimpse of broad shoulder here or a glimmer of his velvety baritone there. He'd communicated primarily via email or text. If she didn't know better, she'd almost think he was avoiding her.

At the restaurant, he'd surprised her. The Lucas she'd seen before that night exuded a steadiness and, well, she had no clue what he was passionate about besides work. But then the set of his chiseled jaw--had she noticed just how strong his jaw was before--and the fire in his eyes hadn't been quiet or calm. He'd had a fierceness, a hint of danger, like he really had wanted to plant his large fist in the guy's face.

When she'd gotten home that evening and settled into her evening wind-down bubble bath, she'd replayed the scene in her mind. Imagined what he looked like beneath the tailored clothes. There was more to Lucas Sutton than what she'd assumed at first glance. And yes, the tips of his ears had flamed red. Definitely his tell.

But now wasn't the time to contemplate Lucas except for as the person who could give her the go-ahead for an exclusive contract. Business came first, and this opportunity was not to be missed.

She'd negotiated an incredible membership deal with The Private Suite, a private luxury terminal serving LAX where guests who could afford it never had to set foot into the chaotic main airport.

Currently the service was available to people individually, but she wanted to broker a deal which featured door to door service to and from the hotel to the private terminal. That way, guests could fly in from anywhere and enjoy luxury meals, amenities, and even spa services. They wouldn't have to even think about the terrible Los Angeles traffic. It could book end their stay at Paramount and none of the other 5-star hotels offered it as part of the reservation.

But she needed to confirm before 8 p.m. tonight or her contact at Private Suite would offer it to The Peninsula or horror of horrors, the Four Seasons. If she had her way, Private Suite would be the first of many unique guest packages she'd create to differentiate Paramount from the rest. So she needed Lucas's approval now.

Determined to track him down, she opened the calendar and her eyes widened. Lucas was at rugby practice at Beverly Gardens Park, near City Hall. The man who never wore jeans was playing a group sport? And rugby? From what she'd seen of the game, it was a bunch of giant men with a ball beating each other up. But who knew? She'd never actually seen a match.

Not that it mattered. He had to take a break for business. When she pulled up the address, she sighed in relief to see it was within walking distance.

Time was of the essence. She grabbed her royal blue cross-body bag and strode out of her office. The contractors had left for the day, and she admired the progress since she'd started. The hotel was going to be magnificent, and she couldn't wait for it to open.

She headed toward Santa Monica Boulevard where the park was located. She savored the late afternoon sun warming her skin. September in L.A. was heavenly so far, with mild daytime temperatures and a crisp coolness in the evening. Nothing like the balmy nights in the Turks and Caicos. It reminded her of the South of France where she'd spent some time growing up.

Although she walked at a brisk pace, she had time to admire a dove gray cashmere sweater in one boutique window and a pair of lime green heels in another. The shopping here was impressive--not Paris, of course, but nonetheless, if she wasn't careful, she could blow through her salary before she earned it. But she preferred to travel light so window shopping sufficed.

She crossed busy Santa Monica Boulevard and approached a small grassy area now dominated by a herd of giants. She stopped and tilted her head. What in the world were they doing? A group of them were in a circle, bent in half, with their arms around each other. Grunts and curses filled the air. Wow.

Because her view was only of muscular derrières and even more muscular pairs of legs, she couldn't tell if any belonged to Lucas. She'd only seen him in slacks, still not even in a pair of jeans. Not that she'd been trying to check out his butt.

"The wives' cheering section is on the other side of the park." A deep voice rumbled from beside her.

She turned and looked up. And up. A giant peered down at her with intense onyx eyes. Good grief, the man was as built like an oak tree. "Wives? I'm not a wife. I'm looking for Lucas?"

He scratched his shaggy dark hair. "Lucas? Lucky guy but don't know who that is. What does he look like?"

"He's tall, but not as tall as you. Red hair. Glasses." Bottle green eyes. Handsome.

The man's broad face broke into a grin, revealing a missing incisor. *Mon Dieu.* "Big Red. He wears glasses? Not here anyway, those would get shattered. He's over there in the scrum."

"Scrum?" She wrinkled her nose.

He cocked his head to the side. "You ever been to a rugby match?"

"No, I haven't." *Would I be asking if I had?* But now wasn't the time for snark.

"That's a scrum." He pointed to the men all still shoving against each other.

Curiosity won out. "And why are they doing that?" While she needed Lucas pronto, this looked like some bizarre ritual usually observed in the wild, with elk or beasts.

"Are you French? My sister married a French guy. His name is Marie." He barked out a laugh.

She nodded impatiently. "Yes, I'm French. The scrum?"

"My brother-in-law isn't talkative either. Is that a French thing?"

When she quirked a brow, he responded, "So when the next play needs to restart, the forwards on one team lock their arms together, like you can see, and they push forward into the opposing side. The ball gets tossed into the scrum and the players try to gain possession by kicking it backward toward their own side. Make sense?"

Not in the least. "I'll take your word for it. Is one of them Lucas?"

"Big Red is right over there, with the gray shorts. He's Number 7." He pointed to a sculpted round butt on sculpted from stone legs.

She drew in a sharp intake of breath. *Oh my.* That was Lucas? His dress pants certainly didn't reveal that he looked like he'd been carved by Michelangelo. "Will they be coming up for air anytime soon?"

He grunted. "Yeah, there's the ball and there they go."

Sure enough, a pack of gladiators sprinted down the field, like they were charging into battle.

If she wasn't mistaken, Lucas had the ball tucked under one muscular arm. The late afternoon sunlight gleamed off his defined muscles as he ran toward the other end of the field. For a moment, she simply admired poetry in motion. He moved like an Olympian. Other guys ran behind him, but nobody could catch him as he sailed across the end zone.

When he crossed the line, he spiked the ball down, threw his decidedly brawny arms overhead and roared "Yes."

He looked like a Greek god after a particularly intense challenge. Sweaty, triumphant, and utterly male. A far cry from a buttoned-up accountant.

Okay, perhaps she had underestimated her boss. Sure, she hadn't underestimated his intelligence or work ethic, but for some reason, she hadn't imagined him being so physical. So in his prime. So delicious.

Cheers and whistles came from some makeshift bleachers where about twenty women were on their feet, waving their arms and hugging each other. It reminded her of how the community was invested in football--soccer--back in France. In high school, she'd had a friend back in Cassis, and she'd always attended his matches. Had loved how close-knit everyone was. Had hated leaving the small town before the school year ended. Hadn't felt that type of group camaraderie in years.

Then, the giant who had been standing next to her lumbered across the grass and bumped him on the shoulder, pointing back to her. Lucas's eyes widened and his sculpted lips parted. But he remained frozen to the spot.

A curl of heat flared low in her belly. Brigitte swallowed and took a moment to compose herself. It was like she'd seen him for the first time. And oh my goodness, how was she ever going to look at him again without seeing him like this?

He jogged toward her, and she struggled not to stare. But she couldn't unsee what she'd seen. What woman wouldn't stare? He was too handsome.

Boss, he was her boss. Her boss she'd promised Charlie to help. She needed to remember that.

His cheeks were red but likely from his run, right? He reached her and tilted his head. "Brigitte? What are you doing here?"

For once in her life, she was at a loss for words. She always had a quick answer and literally, she was speechless. Was this what shy people experienced? "Umm."

"Are you okay?"

"Fine, I'm fine. I had something that I needed to ask you. About work. I didn't know, you, ahem, played rugby." Keep looking at his face, do not under any circumstances stare at the way his t-shirt clung to his chest and revealed the ridges of his abs.

He raked one large hand—had she ever noticed how long and thick his fingers were—through his damp auburn hair. "Yeah, just something I picked up in college and it's a good way to burn off extra energy."

Oh, I can think of better ways. "Oh."

"What did you want to ask me?" He tilted his head. "Are you sure you're feeling okay?"

How had the tables turned, and he was all confidence and she was tongue-tied?

She clasped her hands together and dug her fingernails into her palms. A lifetime of presenting a confident façade took over and she cleared her throat.

"I'm fine. I just need your approval to move forward with a deal I've negotiated for our guests with The Private Suite company at LAX. If we don't sign them tonight, we could lose out to The Peninsula."

He rubbed his jaw for a moment. "Tonight? Isn't that the contract I reviewed? I thought that was up for final approval at the end of the week?"

She nodded. "Yes, it's on one of your spreadsheets. And yes, this is a few days early but as you know, service providers aren't always running by our timetable. And The Peninsula is pressuring them hard."

"Yeah, especially since they're established here and we're not even open yet. This will be a coup if we sign them," he said.

"Exactly. You said you want Paramount to be the best hotel yet. This could do it. One way we'll be able to differentiate ourselves is to have exclusive providers, to add to the value guests receive. We want to offer them something they can't get anywhere else."

"Red, you playin' anymore or flirting?" One of the giants

on the field shouted.

Lucas flipped the guy off, without turning around. But the tell-tale flush immediately appeared on his cheeks.

"Do it. Thanks for taking the initiative and I appreciate you checking in with me prior to signing." His voice didn't reveal a thing.

But the heat in his eyes belied his neutral tone. Damn it, he was mouthwateringly gorgeous. Maybe now that she'd seen this other side of him, he was more handsome? Or she just hadn't looked beneath the surface of his bespoke suits and glasses before.

And she wished she really had not taken it upon herself to follow him down here because now she had a vision stamped inside her eyelids of Lucas Sutton looking like a gladiator. She exhaled a steadying breath--thank goodness for her dark sunglasses because he didn't need to see the flare of attraction she was experiencing.

"Brigitte? You sure you're alright?"

She gathered her composure. "Maybe I'm a little tired, sorry. I'll take care of this. Will you be back at the hotel later?"

"I'll go back to my place first and shower. But yeah, I'll be back in a few hours, it will be a late night."

"Big Red, get your ass over here." Another shout. "Tell your woman to have a seat."

He flashed a crooked grin. "You heard them. Unless you want to be part of the cheering section, you'd better go. See you later."

With that, he turned and sprinted back to the group on the field. And yes, she watched the ripple of his very fine muscles the whole way before turning and marching back to the hotel.

CHAPTER 6

wo Weeks Later--October

BRIGITTE STUFFED her clean laundry into the drawers of her tall armoire. The rest of the team were arriving today, and she was hosting cocktails before the Escape Room. Because nobody needed to see the tornado area that was her two bedroom condo, she'd left work early to clean up.

People assumed she was tidy because she dressed elegantly. If people had any idea how messy she was, her image of the sophisticated Parisian would be ruined. Of course, Charlie knew but she wouldn't reveal her secrets.

Everybody was staying at different high-end Beverly Hills hotels for the weekend, posing as regular guests. Nothing like going incognito to assess the competition. Tonight they'd bond over drinks, the Escape Room, and dinner before putting their heads together to prepare for opening weekend.

The last few weeks had flown by, which was just how she

liked it. Lucas hadn't asked for assistance despite her offer; and unless he was being secretive, everything seemed to be going well. No more sightings of him in workout clothes or even with a ginger hair out of place. Maybe she'd dreamt the scene on the rugby field?

She hadn't had time to dwell on it because she'd been busy coordinating special experiences with everyone from local art galleries to day trips to Malibu, to arranging exclusive shopping hours at high-end boutiques for Paramount guests.

The hotel had been humming with activity and the beautiful interior was emerging day by day, like a butterfly from its cocoon. Through all of it, she'd managed to observe Lucas in action. And she was impressed with his air of quiet confidence and strength.

She hadn't had to step in at all. He'd had no problem managing the contractors who had arrived late, the final interviews with some key front office staff, or the city officials being nosy.

He had a natural reserve but didn't come off as aloof or nervous. Just quiet. And so far it worked. It wasn't like Ryan was the most warm and friendly guy, and he was doing a great job not just as CEO but as G.M. in La Jolla.

What she'd really noticed during her periods of nonchalantly checking in on him was that he had a sharp sense of style. His clothes were meticulously tailored to fit his broad shoulders, tapered back, and narrow hips. Most men who dressed as well as he did weren't built like professional athletes.

She shook her head. No need to ruminate about what he looked like under those suits. If she'd felt an unexpected attraction, she was merely appreciating his male beauty. It didn't mean she had to act on it. Nice, quiet guys were not her type. They tended to want long-term.

She loved men and enjoyed companionship and sex but the minute a guy started getting starry-eyed and suggested going home for the holidays or meeting the family, she was out. It was funny––men always said they didn't want a commitment, or they wanted to keep things light. And the minute they realized she agreed, they would freak out and become possessive or jealous. And off she would go.

Her career choice was a form of natural selection, and it suited her perfectly. She didn't need a partner to complete her. She was perfectly content on her own. Like she'd been most of her life. Just like Charlie had been, until she met Ryan.

A small twinge of unidentifiable emotion tightened in her chest. She was thrilled for Charlie and adored seeing her friend bask in Ryan's love and attention.

But she wondered.

Wondered what it would feel like to have a man truly have her back. To be with a man who was protective and proud at the same time. To meet someone she pictured a future with.

But at 35, she'd never come close. The one time she'd opened her heart at the tender age of twenty-two, she'd had her heart pulverized by an older man. That lesson, compiled upon her nomadic childhood and losing her mother when she was nineteen, forged her commitment to an entanglement-free life.

She blew out a breath, paused with her hands on her hips, and surveyed her high-ceilinged apartment. She'd loved the airy space the moment she'd stepped into it. Wide-planked pale oak floors, enormous windows inviting in tons of sunlight, bright modern paintings strategically hung on celery green walls. It was a cheerful, feminine, and felt like home.

And it just happened to be located across the street from Lucas's place.

The best part?

The rental was a sub-let and belonged to an industry acquaintance who was in Singapore on a one-year gig. Not that she'd been thrilled to have a space with a finite move-out date or anything. Not that she had a built-in escape hatch and could accept the dream position the recruiter had offered her or anything. Denial was a beautiful thing.

She'd arranged a few plates of charcuterie and cheeses, a dish of niçoise olives, and some raw vegetables, which were staying fresh in the stainless steel refrigerator. A few baguettes from the local French bakery were ready to be sliced. Two bottles of Châteauneuf-du-Pape were in the decanter breathing, and some Sancerre and champagne cooled on ice.

Satisfied everything was ready, she hurried back to the large glassed in shower and flipped on the water. One thing she appreciated about America was the big bathrooms and showers. To be able to move around and enjoy flowing hot water was an extravagance she'd never take for granted. Growing up all over Europe, she'd been accustomed to bathing in tiny tubs or shared bathrooms at the end of a dim hallway in the temporary housing she'd shared with her *Maman*.

After toweling off, she slathered on her favorite body cream, savoring the scent of bergamot and ylang-ylang, and the way it melted into her skin. She decided to leave her wavy hair down around her face. It was Friday night, after all, so no need to pull it back into her customary low chignon.

One thing she'd inherited from her mother was her porcelain skin and she took meticulous care of it, so she added a layer of serum and moisturizer to her face and called it a night. She'd wait to add a slick of color on her lips after she dressed.

She wandered into her bedroom and contemplated her closet. Fortunately, she didn't have a lot of clothes, just a few good pieces she rotated. But tonight was casual.

Before she could select an outfit, a sharp knock sounded on the front door. Maybe Charlie had arrived a little early and they could have a few minutes to catch up. She tightened the straps of her short silk robe around her waist, hurried to the front door, and flung it open.

"Lucas, you're early." No, it wasn't her best friend, it was Lucas holding a bouquet of red dahlias. And looking delicious in a pair of dark jeans and a black t-shirt that stretched across his broad chest and emphasized his chiseled arms.

His cheeks flushed and he retreated a step. "Oh, I'm sorry. I can come back."

Before he could turn and hightail it away, she stopped him. "Of course not, especially when you brought me flowers. Thank you, you're so sweet. Come in and I'll get dressed. Pour yourself a drink, the wine's breathing in the kitchen."

He hesitated. "The flowers are a housewarming gift. If you're sure, I don't want to intrude––" He gazed down at the flowers and sure enough, the tips of his ears were darkening.

"Don't be silly. Come in. The rest of the group will be here any minute." The man's bashfulness was irresistible. Some playful part of her took over and she reached for the bouquet, brushing her fingers against his long ones.

A spark of heat raced up her arm and she buried her nose in the fragrant petals to avoid revealing her reaction. Had he felt it, too?

Her apartment was an open plan, so there was no need to lead him to the kitchen, but she carried the bouquet over, locating a vase underneath the wide farmer's sink, and placed it beneath the brass handled faucet. She sensed Lucas behind her.

When she turned with the water-filled vase, he was studying the wine bottle like he'd be sitting for an exam on it any minute. Looking anywhere but at her.

"It's one of my favorites from the Rhone Valley, Halos De Jupiter. I figured I'd splurge for tonight's meeting. Go ahead and make yourself at home. I'll be right back."

He picked up one of the stemless red wine glasses and his lips twitched. "I can officially call this a business expense for our meeting tonight. Glad you splurged."

"I believe in splurging whenever possible. Be right back." So maybe she walked a little more slowly toward her bedroom than she would have if she were alone.

The heat of his gaze seared into her from across the room. No, he'd felt the flash of chemistry when they'd touched. Not that she'd do anything about it except for a little flirtation. Nothing more.

Because she liked Lucas, and she could already tell he wasn't the type of man who did casual. In fact, if she didn't know better, she'd assume he had a sweet little wife tucked away. He seemed like the white picket fence, two children, American dream type of guy. Not in a bad way. Just not her way.

She quickly slid into her Zadig and Voltaire jeans, favorite Petit bateau striped t-shirt, and a pair of red ballet flats.

The doorbell rang and Lucas called back to her. "Okay if I answer the door?"

"Sure, be right there." She applied a quick coat of her go-to 999 by Dior red lipstick and joined him in the living room.

"Hey, Brigitte. You've got Lucas working as your butler

already? Good job." Jack, the handsome G.M. of Maison du Soleil in Paso Robles, waggled his dark eyebrows.

"Very funny. I see your better half isn't here?" Lucas crossed his arms over his broad chest.

Jack shook his head. "Nope, Campbell is in New York for a sommelier conference. But I'm here so we can get this party started. Ryan, Charlie, and Cam are right behind me. Lucy has a wedding that's too big for her assistants to handle, and Austin and Kenzie will be up in the morning."

Brigitte smiled at their obvious ease with each other. "Just leave the door cracked so they can come in. Follow me boys. I'll get the hors d'oeuvres out and the wine poured, and we can catch up."

They made their way into the kitchen area, and she pulled the trays out of the refrigerator. "Lucas, could you slice up the baguette? The knives are in the block over there. Jack, would you mind opening the bubbles? I know Charlie will want to start with champagne."

"Yes, ma'am." Jack saluted. "So how are you liking California so far? Love your place."

"So far, so good. I'm appreciating the lack of humidity and having a little more civilization than the Caribbean. But don't give me too much credit on the place, it's a sublet and came furnished." And don't open any drawers of cabinets where she'd stuffed her clutter.

"Oh wow, how long do you have it for?" He'd already popped the cork and handed her a glass of sparkling liquid.

"Helen's abroad for a year. So it's perfect to get started. The rental market in California is out of control. But as a real estate attorney you know that, right?"

Jack sipped his wine. "Yeah, well in a past life. You should ask Campbell some time about the rental market in Paso Robles."

Lucas snorted. "Yeah, Campbell's got such a soft heart

that she rented out Jack's place before he got there, and he had to sleep on the Murphy bed in her apartment."

Jack's smile was sheepish. "Let's just say it all worked out."

"Well, you are engaged, so I suppose it did." Brigitte tapped her glass against his.

Jack's grin turned sly. "You know how it goes…first Ryan and Charlie…"

"Ryan and Charlie what?" Charlie rushed into the condo and enfolded her in a hug.

Brigitte held her champagne flute up. "Careful with the bubbles."

"Ryan and Charlie, me and Campbell, Cam and Lucy, Austin and Kenzie…" Jack counted off the couples with the fingers of one hand, leaving his pinky finger extended, his pale green eyes twinkling with humor.

Charlie swatted Jack. "Oh stop it."

Ryan and Cam entered and closed the door behind them. "Jack's already causing trouble?"

"When doesn't he stir the pot?" Charlie laughed. "No need to embarrass Lucas and Brigitte."

"Why can't we embarrass Lucas? He's always done it to us. And Brigitte, welcome to the family. No special treatment for you." Cam Taylor, the military veteran with arctic blue eyes, flashed a crooked smile.

Something sharp tugged in Brigitte's chest. These people really were a family, and the unquestioning acceptance was new for her. She liked it a little too much. "No need to handle me with kid gloves. I'm tough and don't embarrass easily, but I have noticed Lucas's tell when he is."

"That's my best friend. And I guess you mean his pink cheeks or his bright red ears?" Charlie winked at Lucas.

Lucas held up a hand. "Hey, it's not kick a ginger day."

"But it's so fun to see if we can make you blush. A big

strapping lad like you. Aren't you ready to walk down the aisle? Maybe with a beautiful French woman?" Jack smirked.

Brigitte choked on her wine. "Okay, Lucas, I'm on your side. Nobody calls you a lad or has me getting married." Even though the "kick a ginger" thing was hilarious, the walking down the aisle was not.

Charlie caught her eye and gave an exaggerated wink. "So you two are a team already, I love it."

Brigitte stiffened. Now that she acknowledged the chemistry with Lucas, what if everyone else did, too? And with the group likely betting on them to get together, no need to throw fuel onto the fire.

"Yeah, it's all going great, but can't wait until Jon gets up here and takes over the Assistant G.M. role. That's probably the best promotion in the company so far." Lucas held his wineglass aloft.

"He's holding down the fort while we're here this weekend and training his replacement but he'll be ready to roll." Ryan stepped up and pressed a tender kiss to the top of Charlie's dark blonde head. Her best friend's lips curved upward, and she turned into her husband's arms.

"We're going to miss that smartass, but he'll be perfect here. He's ready for the promotion, for sure," Charlie said.

Brigitte had adored Jon the few times they'd met. He'd been Ryan and Charlie's right hand person over the last two years. Jon wanted the responsibility and long-term, so it had taken the pressure off her when she'd refused the position.

She topped off everyone's glasses. "Okay, okay, let's all have a toast. Grab some wine and we'll get this evening started. The driver will be here in forty-five minutes to take us to the Escape Room."

Once they each had a full glass and stood around the dove gray marble island, Jack lifted his glass. "I propose a toast to

Paramount being the jewel in the crown of our hotels and to an awesome weekend with you guys."

"To the Hotel Kings and Paramount." They cheered and drank.

Being a true part of a family like this was incredible but likely temporary. Brigitte tucked away the unfamiliar warm fuzziness in her heart. She couldn't allow herself to get too comfortable in case she got her old familiar itch sooner than later. She'd never leave Charlie or any of them in the lurch but her track record of staying around long-term was non-existent.

And as far as she could tell, she was probably too old and set in her ways to change now.

ecause karma was a bitch, Lucas was squeezed in the back row of the party van with Brigitte. Because of course Jack had somehow maneuvered them together, he was one-hundred percent positive. Her lean thigh pressed against his, her mysterious floral scent filled his senses, and if he didn't start silently chanting statistics, a red face would be the least of his problems.

He gripped his legs so tightly that he'd probably leave bruises but that was better than scooping her up and positioning her across his lap. Because giving in to temptation would really make their working relationship go smoothly. Ha.

How far was it to this place?

Brigitte leaned forward and placed one artistic hand on the back of the leather seat in front of them. "Okay, I say we have a wager."

"On the offensive, I love it. You'll fit right in. So, a wager on you and––" Jack said.

Brigitte's musical laugh filled the van. "*Non*, don't be silly,

Jack. This Escape Room tonight has people go through in pairs. I was going to say that the last place team buys dinner."

"It's all on the corporate card. But we could have the losers have to be the ones to fetch coffee and meals all week-end," Ryan said.

Figures Ryan would have the perfect grunt work for the losing team.

"I'll look forward to you bringing me coffee––don't forget I like it with three sugars." Jack elbowed Ryan.

Ryan bumped his shoulder. "And a bowl of cream like a damn cat, yeah, yeah. You wish. Nobody can beat Charlie and me."

Brigitte shook her head, her shiny dark hair gleaming in the early evening light. "No, you and Charlie can't be part-ners. You already finish each other sentences. We need to mix it up."

Cam glanced back over his shoulder. "Well, we've known each other since college and Charlie and Brigitte have known each other for years, too. I think it needs to be a random selection."

Lucas pointed a finger at his friend. "Or how about simple alphabetical order. Brigitte and Cam, Charlie and Jack, and me and Ryan."

Brigitte's lips twitched. "I thought you specialized in numbers, not letters?"

"Order is order." He returned the smile. Now if they could get to the place before his brain totally shut off from her proximity.

Charlie clapped her hands together. "Love it. And were you going to tell us what type of room it is or are you going for a surprise?"

Brigitte shrugged. "I found one that is on point for us. It's a haunted hotel and the goal is to solve the crime so the ghost who was murdered can finally be at rest."

Charlie barked out a laugh. "That's the one thing we didn't check for when we acquired all the properties. The Monroe in Palm Springs opened back in the 1930s and wasn't yours originally built around the same time? Maybe you guys will have the ghost of some silent screen star or something."

Lucas frowned. "No way. If anyone has a haunted hotel, it's Austin with The Monroe. But anyway, this sounds like a good distraction from work."

"That's exactly why I chose this because I know we'll be deep in it all weekend. Plus, it's a good brain exercise, too, you really have to focus but also think outside of the box. And it's fun." Brigitte turned the full force of her smile on him.

His throat tightened and so did his jeans. Yeah, he definitely needed to have something to focus on besides her. Thank god they weren't going to be partners because he needed some space. And he'd make sure they weren't sitting together on the way to dinner. He was man enough to admit that he needed to have some breathing room to resist her.

The driver pulled up to a small gatehouse outside enormous wrought iron gates and the security guard asked, "It's the Michaels group, right?"

"Yes, thank you. Michaels, party of six," Brigitte called.

The van navigated down a winding, tree-lined drive. The path opened up to a wide clearing and then the structure appeared.

"Holy crap, it looks just like that hotel Stephen King used as inspiration for *The Shining*," Jack smacked the back of the seat in front of him. "This is awesome."

"You're right, it's just like The Stanley out near Rocky Mountain National Park in Colorado. It really does look like pictures of it, doesn't it?"

Brigitte pressed a hand to her chest. "I'm not familiar

with those but they did say it would look like a hotel from a famous movie."

It was Lucas's turn to be shocked. "You've never read or seen *The Shining*? Are you serious?"

Brigitte's dark eyebrows drew together. "I've heard of it, of course, but I don't like horror films or books."

"And you chose a haunted house with a murdered ghost?" Jack laughed.

She shrugged and her smile was slightly sheepish. "Fair point. I guess I didn't think it would be that scary, more creepy. I was more focused on it being a hotel."

"We're here, kids." Ryan opened the sliding van door and reached one hand out to help Charlie descend to the pavement.

In the first break he'd had tonight, Lucas was able to exit the vehicle before Brigitte. He sucked in a deep inhale of the crisp evening air.

Jack stepped up and smacked him on the back. "You good?"

He nodded. "Yeah."

"It will help when Jon's up here full-time. I remember how much I had to juggle opening Maison du Soleil. And we'll get stuff sorted tomorrow. Remember you can delegate, and you can always call me, okay?"

Lucas stiffened. "I think you called me one time during your pre-launch, and it was for something in my financial role. I know you guys are busy now the hotels are all open. It's different."

Jack's brow furrowed. "Come on, don't be ridiculous. Your success reflects on all of us. We're in this together."

And that's exactly the issue--if he fucked up, it reflected on the whole chain of hotels. It would be the first time he failed his best friends. It was a double-edged sword being the last hotel to open. His gut twisted but he forced himself to relax--nothing to be done about it tonight.

"Stop gossiping, you two. Let's do this," Charlie strode toward the entrance stairs of the imposing building. "I want to find out who turned this place into an Escape Room."

They headed toward the solid twenty-foot tall doors with enormous brass lion doorknobs.

Just as they'd crested the creaky top stair--nice touch-- the doors opened from the inside, but nobody was there.

They walked into the vast space that must have been the lobby, back in the day. Two enormous spiral staircases framed a set of double doors. Burgundy flowered wallpaper peeled off the walls, rusty sconces flickered, and a dampness hung in the air. The entire structure appeared to be constructed of wood, and rafters covered with cobwebs and maybe even a few bird's nests yawned above them.

"*Mon Dieu*, look at the hole in this ceiling," Brigitte exclaimed as she spun in slow circle.

Lucas glanced up and sure enough, there was a jagged opening that revealed the twilight sky. Hell, if a colony of bats descended upon them, he wouldn't be shocked.

"Let's hope we're not using the same contractors," he said.

Cam chuckled and pointed at him. "Look at that, Lucas made a joke."

"Hey, again, it's not kick a ginger day." Lucas flipped him off. He could be funny.

Before Cam could respond, a woman in an old-fashioned 1940s style wedding dress materialized through the double doors. "Hello there, you must be the Michaels party. We're ready for you. If you're sure you still want to proceed."

Brigitte approached her. "Of course we're sure, why wouldn't we be?"

The youngish blonde woman gave a Mona Lisa smile. "Sometimes people come in and decide against venturing further into the hotel. But of course, you all look like you're brave enough to try to solve the murder. Please gather around and I'll give you your assignments."

Ryan rolled his eyes. "Here we go."

Charlie elbowed him. "Play along. It's all part of the experience."

The woman paused dramatically before diving in. "On a stormy night in March 1933, a young actress named Dorothy Gable was murdered here. There were several suspects, but her killer was never found.

"She had a fiancé, a handsome co-star she was rumored to be having an affair with, a female assistant who was supposedly in love with Dorothy's co-star, and an unhinged movie director who began to believe Dorothy was actually the character in the movie he was directing. They all had alibis. But Dorothy's ghost has been seen here every time someone tried to buy and renovate the property. She chases off anyone who tries to change it. We believe that she cannot leave to the great beyond until her killer is named. So, that's your assignment tonight––to set her free.

"The hotel rooms are full of art and precious collectibles, there are drawers full of old letters and photos, which you can use to piece together what really happened here that night. And, in order to get out and win, you must tell us who the murderer is. You will have ninety minutes. Any questions?"

"If we're going through in pairs, are we going at a staggered pace or do we all start at once?" Lucas felt his competitive edge rising to the surface. This would be a good distraction from his attraction to Brigitte. At least for a few hours.

"Excellent question. There are three different starting points, so you will each start in a different room and move through that way. It is possible you'll cross paths, but you may not." She paused and looked down at her clipboard. "I have your assignments if you are all ready to begin?"

Brigitte shook her head. "Oh, we already chose our teams."

The Mona Lisa smile again. "That's not how it works. So, the first pair who will start in Room A is Jack and Ryan. Room B is Charlie and Cameron, and Room C is Brigitte and Lucas."

Lucas ground his molars together. If he didn't know better, he'd figure Jack engineered the pairs to throw him and Brigitte together again. But without looking like a total dick, he couldn't protest.

Ryan shrugged. "It's fine everyone. Look at it this way, you could have gotten stuck with Jack, like I did."

"Very funny, we all know I'm the smartest one here. We're going to win." Jack laughed. "Let's do this."

Charlie stuck her tongue out at Jack. "You wish you were the smartest. You two don't have a chance."

The woman produced three envelopes and handed one to each of them. "The timing starts now. If you make it through I'll see you again. As long as Dorothy thinks you're trying to help her, you should be fine."

Brigitte, seemingly unaffected by the team switch, winked at him. "Shall we?"

When Brigitte turned the doorknob into the first room, the surroundings changed dramatically. They entered a perfectly preserved library, complete with a fire roaring in a massive stone fireplace, floor to ceiling mahogany bookcases, and a crystal decanter of liquor and two glasses sitting on a low mahogany table.

Lucas whistled and looked around. "Wow, it really is like stepping into a movie set, right?"

Brigitte nodded and sprinted over to an enormous roll-top desk. "Aha, the drawer with letters and photos. Let's start here."

He strode to the shelves and ran his hand along the books' spines. They were all perfectly preserved leather-bound books ranging from classics to more obscure titles. "We should add a small library at Paramount. This is incredible."

"I agree. Maybe a nook sitting area in the main lobby that can be partitioned off slightly or something?"

"Adding some shelves shouldn't be a problem. Unless we have to consult Dagmar."

Brigitte laughed. "No, we'll have Travis draw up the plans; Dagmar will never know the difference. Or we can blame it on the architect."

"Aha, I like the way you think." And look.

"Lucas, come look at this." She waved a cream-colored sheet of paper that was yellowed at the edges.

He crossed to the desk, and together they read a sentence that was written in a spidery script. "Bram Stoker lights the way."

A small line formed between her eyebrows. "Now it's a vampire story?"

"No, maybe something is hidden in the book? I know I just saw it?" He hurried back to the bookcase and pulled the copy of *Dracula* bound in a deep burgundy hue from the shelf.

And with a soft whirring noise, the bookcase opened inward to reveal a shadowed tunnel, with dimly lit sconces mounted high on the walls.

Brigitte joined him in the entrance, her eyes wide. "What in the world? A hidden passageway? This place is beyond what I could have imagined. It's more murder mystery than escape room."

"I'd say so. Let's review the letters and photos first and

then head down it."

They spent ten minutes rifling through the documents, but nothing appeared to be a clue.

"I believe these are what you call the red trout, right? To distract us."

Lucas barked out a laugh. "You mean red herring?"

A crease appeared between Brigitte's dark brows. "Don't laugh at me. You have no idea how many bizarre idioms and phrases there are in English. I cannot keep up with them all."

"I'm sorry. I'm not laughing at you. It's cute."

"Cute? Did you just call me *cute*?" She advanced on him brandishing a pearl-handled letter opener.

More like fucking breathtaking. And the little mistake just made her more human, less an out of reach goddess. "Cute is a compliment."

She shook her head. "*Non*, cute is what you call kittens or puppies."

He held up both hands. "Apologies. But it was meant as a compliment. We should go down the tunnel. We'll close it behind us in case someone comes in. No need to give anyone a leg up."

"Agreed." She set the letter opener back onto the antique desk, squared her shoulders, and marched to the doorway.

They stepped into the passageway and immediately the temperature dropped to downright frigid. Which was quite a feat in Southern California. Once again, her alluring scent filled his nostrils and the warmth from her skin contrasted to the chill. He stuffed his hands into his pockets before he reached out and did something stupid, like stroke her shiny hair or catch her hand.

Making sure he kept a safe distance between them, he led the way down the winding hallway. "Stay close behind me and let me know if you notice anything that could be a clue."

Suddenly a loud noise sounded behind them, and the wall

lamps flashed off without warning and plunged the tunnel into utter darkness.

Brigitte gasped and stepped closer to him. "Lucas, I don't like this."

Neither did he but no way would he admit it to her, especially when she sounded genuinely rattled. A flash of adrenaline shot through him despite knowing this was an Escape Room, designed to distract them from winning the challenge.

"Don't worry. I'm sure the tunnel leads to another exit and if it doesn't, we should be able to open that bookcase again." He injected a note of confidence he wasn't feeling into his voice.

An icy breeze wafted over them, and Brigitte wrapped her fingers around his wrist. "Lucas, where is that draft coming from?" Her voice wavered.

A wave of protectiveness filled him, and he pulled her in closer. "I'm not sure but they're probably blowing it in for effect. Let's keep moving down the passage. There's got to be a clue or another doorway soon. Remember, we've only got ninety minutes, so something has to be close."

It damn well better be.

CHAPTER 8

O kay, she was officially losing it. This experience was nothing like the lively Escape Rooms she'd enjoyed in London. This was downright creepy--what had she been thinking?

Her skin was chilled, her heart hammered against her ribcage, and her breath was coming in sharp bursts. Being in the black tunnel was triggering one of her worst memories and she wanted out. Now.

Lucas turned and tugged her against his firm--very firm--side. His crisp, masculine scent and his sheer size beside her instantly soothed her. A little bit. He kept one arm around her, fished his phone out from his back pocket, and flipped on the flashlight.

"Brigitte, you're shaking. I've got you, okay?"

She gazed up at him, unable to make out his features in the darkness. "Maybe I should have mentioned I've got a bit of an issue with dark enclosed spaces." *Or more accurately, I am terrified of dark enclosed spaces.*

"Just take long, deep breaths. The phone light will guide us. We'll be out of here and onto the next phase of the game soon. I'm sure this is all part of the experience to make everyone feel like this place is actually haunted." His deep voice was reassuring.

She shivered but nodded her head. "Okay." Although she really wanted to sprint back, shove that bookcase door open, and return to the study.

Why in the world had she chosen a haunted hotel again?

"You okay with me holding your hand?" Lucas's voice was husky.

"*Oui.*" Although the panic clawing at her chest wasn't subsiding.

He intertwined his thick strong fingers with hers. She squeezed his hand, not ashamed to need the connection in the dark. The heat from his palm and his solid frame comforted her as they navigated into what felt like a black void.

"So tell me how you and Charlie first met."

Her lips curved upward. He was trying to distract her. Sweet man. "We bonded over catching our doctor with his mistress back when we worked at a fancy hotel in Miami about ten years ago."

He made a choking sound. "What?"

Focus on the story and not on the sweat prickling on her forehead. "So we both had the same dermatologist, which is someone you really need when living in Miami and later in the Caribbean. He was a seemingly nice older gentleman with photos of his lovely wife and children all over his office. So one day Charlie and I were working the front desk and I handled a call for the concierge––"

"Were you two working reception?"

"Yes, like Ryan, we both worked our way up the ladder. I took a phone call for a guest who wanted to have rose petals spread on the bed in his room and a bottle of expensive champagne on ice. When he told me his name, I almost died because I realized it was Dr. Mendez. But I assumed it was a surprise for his wife, their anniversary perhaps."

"And let me guess, it was not."

They continued walking, Lucas's flashlight illuminating a narrow path. But now she was fully in the memory of the story and her breath was regulating.

"*Non*, not even close. Later that afternoon, in strolls the doctor with a 6 foot model, built like a gazelle with waist length blonde hair. Definitely not his wife. He caught sight of Charlie and me behind the reception desk and turned white as a ghost."

"Hey, no talk of ghosts, remember?" He squeezed her hand. "What happened next? Did he check in?"

Between relaying the story and his steadiness, she'd momentarily forgotten about her nerves.

"That's the funny thing. He turned and went to check in with Marco, who was manning the other desk. He pretended like he hadn't seen us, but we know he had."

"So he just went in there with another woman in front of you? What, he figured your doctor/patient privilege applied?"

Brigitte giggled, and she wasn't generally a giggler. "You're funny. He probably figured what could we do? But hold on, the best part is coming.

"About forty-five minutes later, he hightailed it through the lobby, skirting around the other side of these huge marble columns. Maybe we spooked him."

Lucas laughed. "Serves the cheating bastard right."

She tilted her head up toward his in the shadows. "It sounds like you feel strongly about it."

"Hell yeah I do. A real man or woman, for that matter, doesn't sneak around on their partner. If they want out of the relationship, just leave." Disgust filtered through his tone.

"Who wants that type of complication? Keeping it simple

is the best policy--one person at a time." Whenever she dated someone, no matter how briefly, she was with that person. When she got bored, as she invariably did, she moved on. No harm, no foul.

"Agreed."

The winding hallway narrowed drastically and now they could barely squeeze through without their shoulders brushing the walls. Her mouth went dry, and her heart raced again as the walls literally closed in. Maybe they should turn back.

They rounded a sharp corner and the outline of an arched door appeared. "Oh, maybe we can finally get out of here." *Keep it together a little longer, girl.*

"I'll break that door down if I need to. We're almost there."

Suddenly, a gate dropped from the ceiling directly behind them, effectively trapping them in the tiny space between it and the formidable looking door.

A flash of heat streaked through her, and tiny dots danced across her vision. A wave of nausea flooded her body, and she couldn't breathe. Her legs began to crumple.

"Brigitte, Brigitte!" Lucas's deep voice came from some-where faraway.

Everything went black.

BRIGITTE SHOOK her head and forced her heavy eyelids open. Lucas's strong, chiseled jaw was mere inches from her face. He cradled her against his solid chest, his powerful arms holding her close. Her breath lodged in her throat, and she shifted instinctively.

He tightened his hold. "I've got you." His voice was husky.

"What happened?" The last thing she remembered was

her vision dimming. Oh, *Mon Dieu*, she'd fainted. Shame flowed through her.

"You started to go down, but I caught you before you hit the ground." He stroked his thumb across her cheek. "How do you feel?"

She blew out a breath. "Like a fool. You can put me down, I'm fine." And despite her embarrassment, heat blossomed low in her belly.

He hesitated for a moment and kept one arm cradling her against his chest and slowly lowered her legs to the stone floor. "I've got you. Just hold onto me until you feel steadier."

Something tightened in her chest at his protective, almost possessive tone. She was accustomed to men being physically attracted to her but not so much with one wanting to take care of her.

She pressed one hand against him and the temptation to stroke her hand along his hard muscular chest was overwhelming. He smelled delicious, like clean laundry and hot male. The air between them thickened.

She lifted her gaze and drew in a sharp inhale. His eyes were hooded, his jaw tight, his handsome face tense.

"Brigitte," he rasped.

Unable to resist, she wove her arms around his strong neck, and stepped in closer. "Kiss me."

With a growl, he backed her up against the wall, slid his hands into her hair, and slanted his mouth against hers. Her lips parted. Surrendering. Eager to taste him. Their tongues danced and stroked, and she melted into his fiery, demanding kiss.

She curled her fingers into his shirt, and his chest rumbled. He stroked his hands down to grip her hips, tugging her against him. She rocked her hips against him. He pressed kisses along her jaw and grazed his teeth along the sensitive skin on the side of her neck. Liquid heat curled low in her belly.

"You're the most beautiful woman I've ever seen," he murmured against her collarbone, his warm breath caressing her skin.

He lifted his head and gazed down at her, his green eyes gleaming like a cat's in the shadows. Her breath came in sharp bursts, lost in his intense attention.

She stroked one hand along his jawline, "You're nice." Although between seeing him on the rugby field all sweaty and rugged, and the way he kissed, he was much more than that. But she needed to regain control here and not let this spiral. Especially after fainting in his arms, like some Victorian damsel.

He cupped her breasts, stroking his thumb across her tight nipples. "Does that feel nice to you?" he rasped.

She arched into his powerful touch, savoring the sensation rioting through her system. Oh who cared, she wanted more. Needed more. She drove her fingers into his thick, silky hair and tugged his mouth back to hers. Their tongues tangled and he lifted one hand to the back of her head, holding her firmly in place while he dove deeper.

A sudden thumping on the door jolted them apart. "Anybody in there?"

They stood there panting, and she pressed her fingertips to her swollen lips, struggling for composure.

"Shit, it's Ryan." Lucas muttered and adjusted his pants.

She exhaled and smoothed her hair back from her face. "We've got to open it, right?" She whispered.

He nodded, his lips pressed into a firm line. "Hold on, we don't even know if we can. Can you open the door from that side?"

"Do you think I'd be banging on it if I could? The clue on the door says to knock." Ryan's tone was irritated.

Lucas turned to her. "You okay?"

Her legs were wobbly, and he'd practically blown the top of her head off with his passionate kisses but, sure, she could handle it. "*Oui.* Please don't say anything about what happened." Not the fainting. And definitely not the kissing.

He stared at her for another beat, gave a sharp nod, "We will discuss what happened."

He turned and examined the door. "Ryan, there are like ten locks on here so give me a second, you cranky bastard."

"Don't call me cranky, I'm your boss." Ryan laughed.

"Those two things are not related." Lucas crouched down and tugged open the first of several deadbolts.

The soft material of his shirt stretched across his broad shoulders and even in the shadows, the definition of his chiseled muscles was visible. And now she knew for sure that every inch of him was hard, from his defined pectorals, down the ridges of his abdominals, to his impressive erection.

She curled her fingers into her palms, working to restore her usually insouciant attitude. Nobody could suspect anything had happened between her and Lucas. They were all betting on the two of them hooking up and she refused to give them the pleasure of being right, or the money, for that matter.

And just as important--nobody needed to know about her fear of enclosed spaces. Ever.

Nobody needed to know how Lucas's protective streak made her feel warm inside.

No, what happened in the passageway would remain between her and Lucas. She was really building up the secrets in the short time she'd joined the Hotel Kings, but it couldn't be helped. First with her best friend and now with her boss.

Now that she was getting to know Lucas better, she had a feeling he would be pissed to learn that Charlie had asked her to help him. He was more than competent, he just needed to learn to deal with some of the more difficult personalities without letting it ruffle him.

"Here we go," Lucas said and opened the door.

Light flooded into the space and Brigitte shaded her eyes with one hand, blinking a few times against the sudden glare.

They entered a high-ceilinged lemon colored room with an antique four-poster bed with a lush emerald velvet coverlet, a tall stone fireplace with a roaring fire, and plush patterned carpeting.

"Wow, it looks like this room has been completely preserved." Lucas crossed the room in long powerful strides.

Ryan smirked. "Yeah, this is supposedly Dorothy's bedroom and where her ghost"—he made air quotes–"floats around and builds fires."

Brigitte put her hands on her hips, thrilled to have something to distract her. "What I don't understand is how would they know someone would be in the tunnel to open the door? And have you run into Charlie and Cam?"

Jack spoke from the open doorway. "That tunnel is unnerving as hell. Was it pitch black like that the whole time? Did you guys solve the mystery yet?"

Lucas pointed at him. "No, the lights went out. And, like we'd tell you. Brigitte and I are winning this thing. You'll just have to figure it out yourself."

Jack's unusual jade green eyes narrowed. "On that note, Ryan, let's get going. And as for the door question? They had us all start in different rooms so, who knows?"

"C'mon, let's go. We're winning. Let these two try to figure out this room." Ryan strode to join Jack. "See you kids on the flip side. If you make it out."

And with a smirk and a slam of the door, they were gone.

Brigitte pivoted to look at Lucas, who was studying some of the old-fashioned portraits hanging on the wall.

"Find anything?"

He continued to scrutinize the frames and shook his head. "Not yet. But it must've been hard for her to sleep in here with these guys all staring at the bed."

She laughed. "Fair point. Well, let's see if I can find the clue in here. We better hurry."

He glanced down at his watch and his eyebrows drew together. "Damn, we've only got 30 more minutes to solve this. We'll work together but what are we looking for?"

She flung open the ornate doors of the tall mahogany armoire against the far wall, revealing rows of silks and taffetas. "I'll check in here. Maybe some of her dresses had pockets or had something sewn inside. Why don't you look in the nightstands?"

Lucas strode to the one against the far wall, placing him on the other side of the bed. He yanked open a drawer and rifled through the contents while she ran her hands along each dress, searching for a clue.

The game helped her compartmentalize. Lucas's protectiveness. Lucas catching her when she fell. Then the kiss that had almost caused her to faint again--from desire, not fear. The sooner they could rejoin the group and head to dinner, the better.

The lights blinked and bells chimed. What now?

Brigitte's phone buzzed and she pulled it out of her purse.

> Cam and I solved the crime! Meet us down in the kitchen. We're here plotting all the chores the rest of you can complete this weekend.

> Well, who did it?

Brigitte wanted to find the killer.

It was the fiancé after he discovered Dorothy was having an affair. Hurry back here—this place gives me the creeps.

After responding with a thumbs-up, she turned to Lucas. "It was the jealous fiancé after he found out Dorothy was cheating. Let's go."

He studied for a moment, in that steady way of his. "Are you sure you feel okay?"

"I'm fine. Let's just act like nothing happened, if you don't mind." The fainting *and* the kiss.

A muscle in his chiseled jaw twitched. "Of course. Let's go."

Together they found the way down the staircase to meet everyone. If her legs still trembled and her heart raced, it was likely an after-effect from her fainting. That's all.

CHAPTER 9

"We've reviewed every single contract, permit, potential disaster, and beyond. That's every-thing, right?" Lucas leaned back in his chair and surveyed his living room.

Everyone was spread around the open space, on chairs, the couch, and Kenzie and Austin cuddled on the floor beneath the enormous picture window. Business as usual with the most incredible team, no, the most incredible family he could imagine.

Now it was Sunday afternoon and they'd been going non-stop since yesterday morning. He'd managed to maintain his distance from Brigitte, who sat across the room with Charlie and Ryan. Thank god because after her scaring the hell out of him when she'd collapsed in his arms, followed by their kiss, he was having a tough time processing the unfamiliar feel-ings bombarding him. Which was vital if he was going to keep his head in the game.

"Great job, Lucas. I think we've been more than thorough. I think the only remaining issue is the special permit for the outdoor dining. Did Fast Facilitators ever get back to you about rescheduling?"

Lucas gritted his teeth. "Yeah, not exactly. Brigitte did get through to another partner though so one of them is supposed to come by soon because we're getting major push-back from the Community Development Department. We've got another time scheduled this week." *But he wasn't holding his breath.*

"You'd think the city would be eager to issue it after the increased popularity of dining outside. It will all work out." Ryan turned to Brigitte.

"And Brigitte, Charlie didn't exaggerate your skills one bit. If I hadn't already given Jon the Assistant G.M. role, I'd try again to convince you to take it."

Brigitte's full lips curved upward. "Thank you, I'm happy to help but you know I would turn you down again."

A crease appeared between Charlie's eyebrows. "Ryan's right, you'd be incredible in management. You've made the move out here to California, you're one of the family now. Don't you want more?"

Brigitte shrugged and looked at her best friend. "You're right—I am here. Why do we need to make it more than that? You know I prefer the freedom of being concierge and I'm excellent at it."

Charlie frowned. "I thought you wanted freedom until you found your forever place."

"I've never had a forever place." The tightness of Brigitte's jaw belied her light tone.

"We'll discuss this later." Charlie crossed her arms and sat back.

Brigitte waved a hand. "Please continue."

Not sure what that was about except maybe Brigitte might be looking at her job as more of a short-term gig? And why did that make his gut tighten? He tucked away the flash of palpable tension between Charlie and Brigitte to analyze later, along with his seeming inability to stop fixating on all things Brigitte.

After dinner Friday night, the guys had given him shit about how well they seemed to be getting along. That was the problem with working with people who knew you better than anyone else. He couldn't exactly hide from them.

And now he knew how she tasted. How soft her skin was. How she made little purring sounds in her throat when he touched her. And no way in hell was he going to be able to compartmentalize that--at least not yet. Maybe if he could have a couple day reprieve without having her in such close proximity, he'd pull it together.

And judging by how nonchalant and breezy she'd been acting all weekend, he was the only one affected. She didn't seem fazed in the least. She'd said hello like everything was the same as before the kiss, which it definitely was not, and basically ignored him except for necessary participation in work discussions.

Was he the only one impacted by their chemistry? Maybe she was embarrassed that she'd shown a moment of vulnerability when she fainted? Or maybe she could flip it on and off like a switch?

He gave himself a mental shake of the head. Work--focus on finishing strong. He addressed the team, "Thanks for doing this today. Everything is on track better than expected. I couldn't do it without you."

"Dude, we're in it together. It's been the same deal with all our hotels. You went above and beyond for me and for everyone else. No reason your experience should be any different," Austin said.

"And there are bets on *all* those experiences." Jack smirked.

"Jack, stop it." Charlie barked out a laugh. "Lucas and Brigitte aren't going to be a couple. Never in a million years."

Lucas tensed--what was that supposed to mean? Why would Charlie be so certain they wouldn't? Why did he feel mildly insulted at her assumption? Not that he wanted them to bet on them.

He caught Brigitte's gaze, and she subtly shook her head. Like he was going to say anything to the group. Because no way was he going to admit they'd kissed and judging from the way she'd acted all weekend, she felt the same way.

"What? Why should they get special treatment? I mean, you and Ryan were a long shot and everyone else has been the subject of bets. Now I can't joke about how much money we have riding on them?" Austin laughed.

Lucas flipped him off. "Hey, standing right here. If you're finished being a child, we can wrap this up."

Brigitte held up one elegant hand and surveyed the room. "Hold on a minute, just how much money is involved and who bet what?"

Crickets.

Cam cleared his throat and shot Lucas an apologetic glance. Lucas knew damn well that every single one of them had wagered. And granted, he was guilty of doing the same for the others. For some reason, now he was in the hot seat, it wasn't as funny.

When nobody responded, Brigitte said, "Well, Lucas and I have been sleeping together for weeks now, so if you've all bet the same way, does that mean we get the money?"

The room erupted and Charlie leapt to her feet. "What?"

Lucas's jaw dropped. What the actual fuck? "Brigitte, you know that's--"

The front door clicked shut. He checked his watch-- damn, his parents were already here. Because they knew everyone was in town, they had insisted on coming by to say hello before taking him to dinner tonight. Although they only lived a few hours away, he didn't see them as often as he liked.

"Hello everyone, it sounds like we arrived at an interesting time." His tall, red-haired mom stepped into the room. "And now I must meet Brigitte."

Lucas's dad wore his poker face, and he stepped in and clapped a large hand on his shoulder. "Yes, son, why don't you introduce us?"

And the last thing he needed was for them to overhear this conversation. His mom had been pestering him to get married and give her grandchildren for the last decade. No need to get her hopes up.

Damn it. He'd never hear the end of this from his parents. The back of his neck blazed, and his damn ears were probably in flames. He glanced at Brigitte. What the hell had she been thinking?

Two flags of pink blazed on Brigitte's high cheekbones. Was the woman actually embarrassed? She rose to her feet and sauntered over to where he stood next to his parents, as if she hadn't just dropped a bombshell. A fake bombshell, no less, because if they'd been sleeping together for weeks, he'd be feeling a lot more relaxed right now.

BRIGITTE FORCED a smile and approached Lucas and his parents. Crap, sometimes she really did have a big mouth. Why did they have a key to his condo? Because they'd just walked in without warning.

The whole room buzzed, her best friend was staring at her like she'd never seen her before, and steam puffed from Lucas's ears.

Should she claim she'd just been joking? That would be

the right thing to do.

Or, if she acted like nonchalant, maybe the group would stop with the innuendos and leave her and Lucas in peace. If they believed they'd already hooked up, maybe they would drop it. And she hadn't confided in Charlie about her fainting in Lucas's arms or Friday night's mind-blowing kiss. It wasn't like she was purposefully keeping secrets from her best friend. Only because they'd been working all weekend. *Sure.*

Time to brazen it out. "Hello Mr. and Mrs. Sutton, I'm Brigitte Thibault." She extended a hand to Lucas's mother first.

Lucas's mom gave a firm handshake, her gray eyes twinkling. "Brigitte, it's so nice to meet you. It sounds like we should be getting to know you much better. And please call me Louise."

"I'm the concierge here for Paramount so I'm sure we'll be seeing each other." Perhaps if she'd had an inkling his parents were expected to show up, she might have kept her mouth shut.

But ever since Friday night, she'd been unable to get him out of her thoughts. Because she'd finally admitted to herself that it had been the most incredible, passionate kiss she'd ever experienced. Maybe it was the surprise at how masterful and commanding he'd been. Maybe it had been the feel of his hewn from steel physique. Maybe it had been simple chemistry.

"Brigitte, I'm Tom." Lucas's dad was built like his son—tall and broad-shouldered, with silver hair and green eyes.

Lucas stood there like a statue—silent and still. But the rest of the group was chattering like a troop of monkeys, so time to set the record straight.

"Nice to meet you, Tom. One moment, please." She spun in a circle. "Okay, I was only kidding so you can stop speculating. Right, Lucas?"

He pushed his dark-rimmed glasses up the bridge of his nose. "Of course she was joking. She's just trying to get you all to drop the bet."

Louise held up a hand. "Although I can suspect what the bet is, would someone please enlighten Tom and me?"

Merde. Brigitte tucked a lock of hair behind her ear. Worked to keep her expression smooth.

After a beat, Jack said, "It started with Ryan and Charlie at Pacific Jewel Inn. They were fighting non-stop, kind of like little kids when they have a crush, so maybe I suggested a bet whether they'd get together. And then these guys did the same with me and Campbell. Then, Lucy and Cam–"

A broad smile lit up Louise's face. "Cam, we're so happy to see you and Lucy back together. So, let's see, you've all found the loves of your lives working together launching your respective hotels. And now my son and Brigitte are on your radar."

Lucas's dad clapped his hands. "Welcome to the family, Brigitte. You'll come to dinner with us tonight so we can get to know you better."

Brigitte retreated a step. "Oh no, I couldn't intrude on your family dinner."

Lucas coughed. "Dad, I'm sure Brigitte has plans. We've worked all weekend without a break."

"You should totally go to dinner with the Suttons, Brigitte. They're the best. Besides, we're all heading home anyway," Charlie said, her dark eyes sparkling.

Hanging out with Lucas's parents was completely out of her comfort zone. *Zut,* it was completely out of her universe. She'd never had her own regular family, and she certainly didn't hang out with the parents of the men she'd dated in the past.

She scrambled for a polite excuse.

Before she could utter a word, Lucas's dad said, "We insist. And everyone is welcome to come. The more the merrier."

Brigitte's shoulders softened, okay, maybe a group dinner wouldn't be too awkward.

But, one by one, every single one of them made their excuses, packed up their things, and said their goodbyes. Damn traitors.

Charlie hugged her and whispered in her ear, "Ummm, way to stir up the room. Is there something you're keeping from me? We will be talking later. I'll call you in the morning." Charlie pointed at her and left with Ryan.

And then there were four. So, she was going to dinner with Lucas and his parents.

"I'll just run across the street to my place and change. Shall I meet you at the restaurant?" That way, she could scoot out early.

No such luck.

"Oh, we'll drive. And you two are neighbors, too?" Louise beamed.

Lucas closed his eyes for a moment. "Mom, Brigitte works for me and we're friends. The apartment is just a coincidence."

"Mmm-hmm." Mrs. Sutton crossed her arms across her chest.

This was too much. Before any more innuendos flew around, she'd make her escape. "Pick me up outside?"

Tom nodded. "We'll pull our car up in fifteen minutes, if that's enough time."

"That's perfect. I'm very tired so don't want to make it a

late evening. I'll see you soon." Without looking at Lucas, she fled.

What had she done with her impulsive words? Dinner with Lucas's parents? Well, now she and Lucas could show there was nothing going on between them.

Despite that kiss.

CHAPTER 10

"*D*id you really need to invite her to dinner? You know this is going to be awkward, right? She was only teasing to make the rest of the team stop. Besides, she's my employee." Lucas turned to his parents.

His mom threw back her head and laughed. "Oh sweetie, I remember Jack's speech about how your company doesn't have a prohibition against dating. You and Brigitte could absolutely be a couple. Everyone else is engaged or already married."

"But maybe I'm not comfortable?" He stalked to the window and raked his hands through his hair.

Damn it, he needed some space from Brigitte. Being around the woman was torture. He needed to pull himself together and having a cozy family dinner with his parents was not the way to do that.

"Well, I just couldn't resist. I think she's awfully clever and knows how to handle you boys. I want to get to know her better. Why aren't you comfortable? Do we embarrass you?" She narrowed her eyes.

"Mom, please. Of course not, but did you consider for a moment you are putting her on the spot?"

His dad waved a hand. "Oh, she struck me as she can handle herself just fine. We're just your friendly parents and if she's part of the Hotel Kings family, it means she's a part of our family now, too. Just like Charlie. Just like Kenzie. Just like Lucy and Campbell. Whether you two have a romantic relationship is not the point. So, let's go."

"When you put it that way"… Lucas grabbed his keys and wallet, and they headed out the door. "And I know she doesn't have a family of her own."

His mom gasped and pressed a hand to her chest. "She's an orphan?"

"Well, Mom, she's a 35 year old woman. We haven't really discussed it, but I know she's an only child and her parents are gone." Not that he knew any details except to say she and her mom had moved around and her father wasn't involved.

"Well, more reason for her to feel like part of all your extended families. Now, we'll drive since we parked right here on the street." They paused in front of his parents' navy SUV. "And there she is. My, she's beautiful, isn't she, Tom?"

"She's a knock-out. Go get her and we'll start the car," his dad said.

Yeah, his parents were having a little too much fun with this. Dinner was going to be a minefield. Now their hope he'd settle down would be rekindled.

When his ex-girlfriend had given him an ultimatum about five years ago, he'd let her go because he hadn't been ready for marriage. And since Evie? He hadn't met anyone who had made him want long term and he wasn't good at casual. It was simple--he either was interested in someone or he wasn't. He wanted what all his friends had found over the last few years, but not yet.

Now, every fiber of his being needed to be focused on

opening Paramount. The job was out of his comfort zone, and he couldn't afford distractions, like dating. Or spending more personal time with Brigitte. Not after that kiss. He inhaled a fortifying breath.

No question: the woman was complicated and dangerous to his equilibrium.

Now he just needed to keep it friendly and professional tonight, especially in front of his parents. If he had anything to say about it, she'd sit on the opposite side of the table.

After the short ride to the restaurant where he basically ignored Brigitte and chatted with his parents, he figured he'd survive the night.

But of course, his parents insisted on sitting next to each other on one side of the tiny booth, which meant he was jammed between the wall and Brigitte. Trapped in way too confined of a space. Her familiar floral scent surrounded him and each time she spoke, she gestured with her artistic hands, reminding him of how those short red fingernails felt digging into his skin.

He gritted his teeth and studied the menu. Maybe if the waiter showed up sometime this century, they could order dinner, and he could go home and take a freezing cold shower. Or hell, drive out to Santa Monica and dive off the pier into the icy Pacific.

When his dad told his favorite corny joke, Brigitte laughed her throaty laugh, and a silky fragrant strand of dark hair brushed him. He adjusted in his seat again, his pants feeling a size too small. He silently reviewed the accounting ledgers for the drywall contractor, desperate to get his body under control before he tossed her over his shoulder and ran away with her.

Because that wouldn't give his parents anything to rejoice about.

Suddenly, that elegant hand was pressed against his forearm. "Lucas?" Her voice was a low purr.

He jolted--her touch sending sparks shooting through his system. Oh, he was in so much damn trouble.

He pushed his glasses back up the bridge of his nose and subtly shifted away from her. Because he wasn't already plastered to the restaurant's wall. "I'm sorry, I was focused on the menu. What?" *Just sitting here trying not to explode.*

"Brigitte asked if we should share an appetizer and I think that's a good idea. What are you going to have, honey? I'm just famished," his mom said.

"Sure." Okay, easy enough question.

His mom tilted her head. "So what do you think looks good? You were studying the menu like you were sitting for your CPA exam again."

Now wasn't the time to mention he had no fucking clue what was on the menu--he hadn't digested a word. He glanced down again. "Umm."

Brigitte saved the day, likely without knowing it. "I've heard the ahi sashimi is fabulous here and would love to try it. That is, if you two like sushi?"

His dad nodded. "We do. Never thought I'd eat raw fish but go figure, right? Let's do it."

With the first stroke of luck he'd had since his parents invited Brigitte to dinner, the waiter materialized and took their orders. And, yeah, maybe he ordered a double whiskey, but he needed some fortification to survive the next few hours.

"So Brigitte, are you planning on staying in the United States or will you eventually return to France?" Uh-oh, his mom's subtle interrogation was starting.

Brigitte stiffened but otherwise didn't react to what sounded like a nosy question to him. Until earlier today, he'd assumed Brigitte was in Beverly Hills permanently. And that cliché about assumptions could bite him in the ass.

"Oh, who knows where I'll end up? Maybe France? Maybe here? Maybe New Zealand? Part of the hospitality business requires flexibility and a willingness to move if the company requests it." She sipped her water.

"But you're working with us now, and we're based in California. I don't think we've got any plans of expanding beyond the state." He angled toward her. Mistake.

She shrugged a delicate shoulder, her face impassive. "Yes, but who knows what the future will bring? I've never limited myself from new possibilities."

"Is that why you didn't take the Assistant G.M. role? Because you're planning on leaving sooner than later?" Tension gripped the back of his neck and his fingers curled around his water glass.

One dark eyebrow arched but her blue eyes were unreadable. "I did mention that freedom is important to me, but I won't leave you in the lurch. I committed to Charlie to come here. I'm hopeful Beverly Hills will be the place that feels like home for me."

"Committed to Charlie? What about your commitment to Paramount and the Hotel Kings?" *Was she really here temporarily?*

His mom's throat cleared. "Lucas, I don't think that's what Brigitte is saying. I'm sorry, maybe I should have asked simply if your family is in France or here with you?"

The waiter appeared with their cocktails, and it took all of Lucas's self-control not to toss his back in one gulp. Brigitte downed half her glass of Chablis, the only indication she was affected. Hell, maybe his mom would continue this line of questioning. Because so far it was proving enlightening and he sure as hell didn't like discovering that Brigitte had one foot out the door already.

Brigitte paused before responding, "Well, my mother raised me, and we moved around a lot when I was growing up. She passed away when I was nineteen, so that was that. Charlie is my only family. I consider her to be my sister and as you know families aren't always related by blood. She's a big part of why I came to California."

His dad said, "I'm so sorry about your mother. You're so right about families. We'd hoped to give Lucas siblings, but it didn't work out that way. And look how he ended up meeting the boys in college. They are all brothers in the ways that matter."

"Thank you. It was a long time ago now. And yes, part of what's so appealing about working here is the relationship between all the guys and now Charlie, Campbell, Lucy, and Kenzie. I'm not used to the level of camaraderie."

"They're definitely a family and now you're part of it. I think it's wonderful you realize how important it is to stay connected to the people you love and also to take the position you wanted, not the one they wanted you to take." His mom toasted her with her white wine.

Brigitte gave a half-smile. "Oh, I don't allow anyone to change my mind once I've made a decision."

His mom laughed. "You know Ryan can be quite intense and Lucas may be the most stubborn of all the boys."

"Mom, we're in our mid-thirties." He narrowed his eyes.

"You'll always be boys to me."

"And on that note, if you'll excuse me, I need to head to the ladies' room." Without sparing him a glance, Brigitte rose and strolled away.

The bands of tension on the back of his neck softened. A five minute break from her proximity was welcome relief. And now he wasn't simply bothered by their physical chemistry, or his increasingly complex feelings for her, now he was bothered that she seemed uninterested in the long-term with Paramount.

While hiring a great concierge wasn't too difficult, especially in this town, he'd assumed she'd moved to California for the long-term.

"So, does she know?" His dad studied him from across the table.

He shook his head and looked at his dad. "Know what?"

"That you're crazy about her?" A smile danced on his mom's lips.

Lucas sputtered. "Crazy about her? I mean she's beautiful but I barely know her. We work together." *Shit.*

He was really close with his parents so maybe they could tell he was attracted to her but crazy about her? Did he have a flashing sign on his forehead? A crush was one thing but was it obvious to everyone around him that his feelings grew deeper by the minute?

His stomach knotted. Had everyone noticed this weekend?

Did Brigitte know?

His dad smirked. "You might be able to fool other people but not us. And how could we blame you? She's intelligent, charming, beautiful…"

"Lucas, she's obviously a wounded bird. You heard what she said about her upbringing. Or more importantly what she didn't say. She's been alone in the world since she was a girl, and it certainly doesn't sound like she had much stability before that. She's built her own life; you can't expect her to change in an instant."

He shook his head. "I didn't say I expected her to change."

"Well, we know you and can see you're attracted to her. I like her for you. Her energy is so light and fun, which is good for you. But that girl needs to feel like someone has her back. That she can trust them to be there for her. You've always had that stability so you can provide it for her." His mom leaned in closer, her gaze intense.

He held up both hands. This conversation was going off the rails. "Whoa, mom. You're getting way ahead of yourself. I have one priority through the end of the year and that's not messing up the Paramount launch."

"Life is short so you've got to grab opportunities or people when you can. Love isn't a distraction, it's a complement to everything else." His father shook a finger at him.

"Oh Tom, you say the sweetest things." His mom turned and pressed a kiss on his dad's cheek.

Brigitte returned. "What did I miss?"

"Not a thing." And with the second stroke of luck he'd had tonight, the server appeared with their meals.

The remainder of the meal passed without further incident. His parents managed to chat about what was happening at home and their plans to return for the soft launch of Paramount.

He focused on his food and kept his responses neutral. After what Brigitte had revealed tonight, he needed time to process. Process what his parents had observed about his feelings. Because if she was planning on bailing sooner than later, he wanted to know. Needed to know. Now.

Of course, he was merely concerned with the smooth running of his hotel. That's what he'd keep telling himself.

CHAPTER 11

*L*ucas snapped his laptop shut, surged to his feet, and stalked to the window. After promising himself he wouldn't hire a pain in the ass prima donna chef, he'd already hired and fired three. Well, Dante--another solo moniker diva who could be Dagmar's twin--had stormed out when he'd dared to suggest he omit one dish on the initial planned menu.

Who knew a chef would be so attached to dandelion salad and so opposed to arugula? Nobody wanted to eat dandelions. At least not at Belcanto, his hotel's restaurant.

Dealing with the dramatic personalities was exhausting. Sure, he could have asked Brigitte to step in and handle the temperamental Frenchman, but he'd hesitated. Maybe he'd been avoiding her since the dinner with his parents but not seeing her all week made him brood about her more. Ridiculous.

They needed to discuss what had triggered her fainting. As her boss, he needed to know if she had a physical issue that might show up during work hours. Another glimmer of protectiveness surged through him. He'd never forget the way she went limp, the vulnerability in her eyes. There was something more to it than her being startled. Something deeper. Something heavy. And he wanted to help.

What had started as a crush after Ryan and Charlie's wedding had morphed into something more. She was the most fascinating woman he'd ever encountered and who knows, maybe somewhere down the line, once the hotel was open, they could explore their undeniable chemistry. But not now.

He had his strengths but juggling work and personal life was not one of them.

His watch buzzed alerting him that his 2:00 p.m. interview had arrived. And the guy better be happy with the Vulcan appliances they'd ordered and installed. Patrice, the prior chef, had pitched a fit and refused to work in a kitchen without Hestan equipment.

Although he wasn't in the mood to deal with yet another privileged, out-of-touch Michelin star master chef, he'd suck it up because otherwise they'd never get on track to open it all, much less earn their own Michelin star.

Where was Brigitte? How many off-site appointments could she have? Last month, she'd offered to help him with the overly emotional people and now she was avoiding him? Because he did need her in this situation.

Maybe if he weren't so stubborn, he would have asked Campbell or Austin to sit in on the interview, even via Zoom. Campbell, as a Master Sommelier, was accustomed to all the snobbery associated with the fine-dining world. And Austin had run a bar in Manhattan after leaving his gig as lead singer of Black Velvet Machine. Both were adept at managing difficult personalities—not his forte.

He gave an internal eyeroll and headed out of his office to the unfinished restaurant where he was meeting Executive Chef Candidate Number Four. Campbell had met the guy before when he'd catered one of her exclusive wine pairing events and she'd sang his praises. And Campbell was particular. Maybe this guy wouldn't be too bad.

Santiago Borba was from Portugal but lived in New York City and Aspen before deciding to live close to the ocean. An undisputed master in the kitchen, he created dishes with a Mediterranean flair, and would be perfect for what they wanted to create. Beverly Hills had some incredible dining options, but Borba's take on some classic dishes was unique. As long as he wasn't an asshole.

Not the highest standard but, at this point, Lucas would take someone with an attitude as long as the guy wanted to make Belcanto the new must-dine location. The restaurant's success was tied to the hotel's success, and it had to be perfect.

When he reached the gaping shell which would be Belcanto's kitchen, a wiry man with a short black ponytail, red pants, and a multi-colored shirt awaited him.

"Mr. Borba?" Lucas strode into the room, hand outstretched.

"Ah, Mr. Sutton, please call me Santiago. Mr. Borba is my grandfather." He flashed white teeth, his brown eyes dancing.

They shook hands. So far, so good. "And call me Lucas. Thanks for flying down to meet with me today. Have you had a moment to look around?"

"Your clerk up front showed me in here and I like what you're creating for the hotel. Even with all the dust, it's obvious it will be elegant here. Very European, which is what I prefer."

Lucas smiled. "Well, that's a start. So what do you think of the space?" Because if the guy hated it, there was no point in wasting time. Granted, they could make some alterations, but the bones of the kitchen set up were not going to change, nor would the appliances. Not when they were opening in two months.

He waved a slim arm around the room. "You chose an excellent spot for the restaurant. It's fortunate you have so many huge windows. In Vegas, the restaurant had no windows. It was like a cave. Terrible."

Score one point for Belcanto and Paramount. "Yes, people can say what they want about Los Angeles, but our weather allows for us to use the outdoors for the ambiance. And we'll have an intimate dining patio."

Santiago pointed at him. "Fantastic. In my hometown of Lisbon, offering al fresco dining is necessary to the success of any restaurant. Another reason why the mountains and the desert didn't suit me. Either freezing or boiling––bah. I love Southern California."

Lucas's shoulders relaxed. Okay, this guy was cool. They navigated through the usual interview questions. They agreed on numbers of kitchen staff and sous-chefs and logistics. Santiago was almost too good to be true. Lucas wasn't worried about trying his food just yet because he'd gotten several references and recommendations.

Now for the ultimate test. They stopped against the far wall where the yet-to-be installed Vulcan range and ovens sat in their oversized boxes. He held his breath.

Santiago nodded, his lips curving upward. "Perfect. This is my preferred brand, and I would have requested them if we had met earlier."

Lucas's breath whooshed out. "Great, that's great. Austin Michaels, who oversees all the restaurant launches, ordered Vulcan for all our restaurants. We like consistency."

Santiago turned to him and winked. "When do I start?"

Lucas laughed, caught off guard by the man's down-to-earth attitude. He was unlike any of the other candidates they'd interviewed, that was for sure.

"I appreciate your directness. It's refreshing. As long as the compensation package works for you, we can draw up the paperwork and bring you on board. The sooner the better because we're planning a soft launch for early December before the New Year's Eve grand opening.

"We'd want you to cater that event. There's a lot for you to create in a short period of time with the menus and whatever you need to do before the restaurant opens."

"I don't believe in playing games. I want to be in Southern California, and I want to be a part of making the hotel and the restaurant the best. I want Michelin stars as quickly as possible, and this is the place."

Lucas extended a hand. "Welcome to the team. I'll have my assistant draw up all the paperwork. When can you start?"

Santiago pumped his hand vigorously. "As soon as we sign. I'm ready to hire and train my staff. I've got a few people in mind. They've worked for me in the past and I know they'd be a fit."

"Well, it will be your kitchen and I'll leave those choices up to you, within reason of course. I'll be in touch by the end of the day with details for signing. Draw me up a list of potential kitchen staff and we can get H.R. working on screening."

Santiago patted him on the shoulder, white teeth gleaming and dark eyes sparkling. "This will be an excellent partnership, I know it. I will speak with you later."

In a flash, Belcanto's new master chef hurried out of the restaurant.

Lucas sank onto one of the chairs around the one table in the unfinished restaurant space. He rested his forearms on his legs, dropped his head in his hands, and heaved a sigh of a relief. One hurdle cleared. Now just to get the damn outdoor dining permit completed.

Filipovich had finally deigned to meet with him today. The prick. Not sure what kind of games the guy was playing or if he was just lazy and irresponsible. In a perfect world, they wouldn't even need the Fast Facilitators' services, but outdoor dining permits were trickier now after the last few years.

"Sutton, there you are. We meetin' today or not?" A loud voice demanded.

Lucas lifted his head and stared at the tall man sauntering toward him. The guy had a face like a weasel, sharp angles and bright obsidian eyes. He had a deep widow's peak, with his chin-length hair slicked back.

Lucas stood. "You must be Don Filipovich?"

"You expecting someone else? You seem eager to get this patio approved so here I am. Let's get it done."

Lucas glanced at his watch. "Our appointment isn't for another hour, but I've got a few minutes now, so let's talk. I understand you can help us expedite the approval?" *Remember the permit. Just get it done*

No way was he taking the guy back to his office. They could stand here in the midst of the construction. The guy approached and a wave of pungent cologne almost made Lucas gag. Filipovich was like some cheap TV villain from an old Hollywood black and white. This was the company's top representative in one of the country's most exclusive cities?

"That's exactly what I can do for you. At a price, of course." He smirked.

Lucas nodded. "Great. We got a quote from your firm several weeks ago when we reached out. We're prepared to move forward. How soon can you get us access?"

Filipovich rubbed his chin. "Oh yeah, there was a little error when one of our clerks sent you that number. We can get you the permit by the end of the month, guaranteed, but it's gonna cost you."

Hackles rose on the back of Lucas's neck. Was this jerk trying to pull a bait and switch?

"Let me guess, cost us more than the number you quoted us?"

"You catch on quick, Gingerbread." The guy smirked.

Anger swelled up in him, but he kept his voice even. "My name isn't 'Gingerbread.' How much do you want?"

"Oh, come on, we can kid around, can't we? I'm sure with that hair and glasses, you've been called a lot worse." He shrugged a narrow shoulder. "Anyway, we need double what we quoted you, or we won't be able to fit you in this year."

Lucas forced a laugh. *I will not let this fucker's taunts get to me.* "Double is ridiculous. We'll pay your initial asking price. Like we agreed. Not a dime more."

Filipovich's eyes narrowed. "I don't think you get it. Either you pay what we're asking, or we won't do it. Up to you."

Maybe it was the asshole's tone of voice. Maybe it was the asshole's insistence on calling him "Gingerbread." Maybe it was the idea that one petty asshole thought he could control how Lucas would manage his hotel.

But he'd stopped being bullied years ago and sure as hell wouldn't be bullied now. Anger filled him. He strode to where Filipovich stood and stared down at him.

"I think you're the one who doesn't get it. I don't respond to threats. We're not paying you and if you don't watch your step, your whole little scam operation will get shut down. Now, get the hell out of my hotel before I throw you out." Years of learning to be non-reactive in the face of threatening personalities served him well now because he hadn't raised his voice.

"We'll see about that. You're going to regret this." Filipovich sneered and pivoted to leave.

"What's going on here?" Brigitte appeared, framed in the restaurant's open doorway, a crease between her dark brows.

"Don't worry your pretty little head about it, sweetie." The asshole raked his gaze from the top of Brigitte's head to her peacock blue stilettos as he darted past her and disappeared.

Brigitte walked slowly toward him. "Please tell me that wasn't the candidate for the Chef de Cuisine?"

Lucas's nostrils flared. "Definitely not."

"Are you okay?"

Lucas turned away from her and struggled to tamp down his temper. He couldn't unclench his fists and his jaw was so tight he was shocked his molars hadn't crumbled. That piece of crap could jeopardize Belcanto's success and in turn impact Paramount.

She pressed one soft hand on the back of his shoulder. "Lucas, please talk to me. What was that all about?"

Her floral citrusy scent filled his senses and his muscles stiffened under her light touch. Since when had he lost all self-control? He took a few steps away from her. He was so angry that he needed to go pound on the punching bag.

Her voice grew sharper. "Lucas, look at me. What has you so angry? Who was that man? And why were you threatening to throw him out?"

He took a deep inhale and held it for a few counts before exhaling a steadying breath. "It was the Fast Facilitator guy we were supposed to meet for dinner."

"Okay. So I take it we won't be using them after all?"

"No." He closed his eyes––now what was he going to do?

"Well, I won't push you to discuss what happened if you don't want to tell me. But we should work on Plan B. We can figure it out."

"There is no Plan B. The Community Development Department is backed up through the Spring. That jerk's company was our chance to pull a few strings and move the permit through the system in time for opening day." And as Paramount's G.M., he was one-hundred-percent responsible.

If he couldn't fix this with the CDD, the opening of the Hotel Kings fifth and final California luxury boutique hotel would definitely not be the biggest or best. Damn it, he had to make this work. And not for the first time, he questioned his decision to transition to G.M.

Right now? He longed for the simplicity of crunching numbers. Sure, all the other guys without the requisite hotel experience had made it work, even Austin who was a freakin' ex-rockstar. And now he wasn't sure he could do it. More importantly, wasn't sure he *wanted* to make it work.

"Do you want me to give Ryan a call?"

His jaw clenched. "Don't call him. I'll handle this." Not trusting himself to keep it together, he strode past her, straight out of the hotel.

He needed some space.

CHAPTER 12

$\mathcal{B}$rigitte smoothed a strand of hair away from her face and swallowed a frisson of nerves. Today, she'd been surprised by the sheer fury on Lucas's face and the hardness in his bottle green eyes. Not that he hadn't looked fierce on the rugby field, but today, Lucas had looked scary––the kind of man you wouldn't want to run into in a dark alley.

Another layer peeled away revealing what lay beneath his generally steady even-keeled appearance. Because she'd been unable to forget how fast he'd gone from caring and protective to passionate and possessive after she'd fainted. Unable to forget that kiss, the way his hands had roamed over her, the firmness of his lean muscular physique.

She shook her head and rapped on Lucas's apartment door. Tonight wasn't about revisiting her attraction to her boss. Tonight she'd find out what caused his anger today and offer her support. And tonight she'd have to manage this unfamiliar fluttering in her belly.

The door whipped open, and Lucas stood framed in the doorway. He wore navy sweatpants slung low on his narrow hips and an ancient San Diego State University T-shirt that highlighted his broad chest. A flare of heat shot straight to her center.

His auburn eyebrows drew together. "Brigitte? What are you doing here?"

She cleared her throat and held up a covered plate. "I thought we could brainstorm a solution for the patio permit and I brought dinner."

"You cooked me dinner?"

She laughed. "Well, actually I made the frittata yesterday so technically I am bringing you leftovers, but my frittata is excellent. Spinach, potato, and tomato."

When he didn't step back and invite her in, she inhaled a fortifying breath. Did he have company?

"Is this a bad time?"

He shook his head, stepped back, and waved her inside. "No, sorry you just surprised me. Come on in and I'll get us something to drink."

She followed him inside, checking out the surroundings, and not how the soft material of his sweatpants emphasized his high, round butt.

Polished hardwood floors and high beamed ceilings greeted her and floor-to-ceiling windows framed the twilight sky and tall skinny palm trees. An enormous chestnut-colored couch sat across from a television large enough to screen movies. A football match played without any volume.

Everything was immaculate. A few framed photographs and a few bright dramatic prints on the pale gray walls, but zero clutter. Even the large kitchen looked like someone had polished every surface and never actually used any of the appliances. Her lips twitched--if Lucas saw the disaster she'd left in her own kitchen, he'd be appalled.

"I've got some really good pale ale or wine. What would you like?"

"I'll try the beer, thanks. Let me just turn on your oven because the frittata tastes better warm." She crossed the room and set the dish on the cream and gold granite island. Food first. Then she'd find out what happened today.

"Sure." He strode to the large stainless steel refrigerator and pulled out two bottles. "Glass or bottle?"

"Bottle is fine."

His mouth quirked up on one side. "I didn't think fancy Parisians drank out of bottles."

"Very funny. I'm not so fancy." She laughed.

He handed her the bottle and his long thick fingers brushed hers, sending sparks dancing along her skin. She snatched her hand back. What was it with this chemistry between them?

He merely quirked a brow. "If you say so. And you obviously have something to discuss, or you wouldn't be here."

"I do." Yes, she was here to help with the hotel and be a friend, nothing more.

"One thing I appreciate is that you're direct and you're honest. So tell me why you're here."

A flicker of unease snaked down her spine. Maybe not totally honest because she didn't believe he'd appreciate her leaving the door open on the dream job offer. But unless she left, he'd never find out, so there was no need to volunteer the information.

"Well, I made some calls to a few friends in Miami who work in local government. My friend Naomi confirmed we should be able to expedite the patio permit ourselves with the CDD. I know it seemed like a good idea to use that company, but she told me there were shysters like that in Florida, too. I think we do a conference call with everyone, brainstorm the exact approach, and get Jack's take on the legal side. We'll get it sorted."

Lucas downed a mouthful of beer and placed the bottle on the granite island. "I really didn't want to pull the others into this situation but you're right. If anyone can get the committee to give us the permit, it's Jack."

"He is smart and quite the smooth talker, isn't he?" Jack had impressed her from the first day she'd met him. And he was a genuinely nice guy.

"Yeah, you two are alike that way."

She shrugged a shoulder. "*Merci.* I'm glad we've agreed to pull him in. It will get done. But I had another reason for coming over."

"Another reason?" He pushed his glasses up on the bridge of his nose.

Oh my god, he was so adorable and was that a flush creeping up his neck? So she wasn't the only one who couldn't forget about their kiss. *Down girl.*

"Well, I think we should discuss the scene I walked into today and, I feel like I should return the favor--"

His jaw dropped. "Return the favor?"

"Well, from the other night. When you caught me when I fainted." Heat rose in her cheeks.

He held up his hands. "I didn't catch you because I wanted something in return. I did it because..."

"Because you're a genuinely nice man and it meant something to me that you were so protective." *And you stood up for me with that jerk at Mastro's.*

"Stop putting words in my mouth. It's not quid pro quo. You don't owe me anything," he rumbled.

She huffed out a breath. "Look, I saw how angry you were today, and it seemed more serious than frustration over dealing with some jerk about permits. I'm a good listener and I wanted to talk if you wanted to get it off your chest."

He rubbed one hand along his chiseled jaw and looked down. "You really don't want to hear about this, trust me."

She crossed to him. "But I do. Will you tell me?"

"I guess I really scared you, didn't I?" His brows knitted.

"Not scared but concerned. I mean, you looked fierce on the rugby field"—and scrumptious and hot as sin—"but this was different."

He studied her face. "You *are* observant. Okay, I'll make you a deal. I'll share what triggered me if you tell me why you get claustrophobic. What made you faint."

Her breath caught. *Merde*, she hadn't seen that one coming. "You drive a hard bargain. Okay. Let's promise to keep this between us." But she trusted him.

"Of course. I'd rather you not share what I tell you with Charlie. Although Ryan knows and probably told her."

"Yeah, those two don't have any secrets but you never know." She glanced at the clock. "The frittata will take about twenty minutes, should we sit down?"

"Yeah. And you go first." He gestured toward the over-sized sofa.

They settled onto opposite ends of the couch and she tucked her legs beneath her. Where to start? She hadn't confided about her issue to anyone except for Charlie and the therapist she'd spoken to after her *maman* died.

She exhaled a shaky breath and clasped her trembling hands together. "Okay. So, I mentioned it was only me and my *Maman* growing up. She tried but just couldn't settle anywhere. We'd move to a new town, or a new country and she'd start a job, start dating some man. She was an artist, and she'd usually find work in galleries––anything to support her painting.

"And every time she claimed the city was the one where she'd be discovered, or the gallery was a long-term gig, or the latest man would be her husband. That she was finally going to give me a papa. Something always went wrong.

"At first, I believed it was the horrible boss or the controlling man. But after the sixth move in as many years, I realized it was her. She couldn't stick." She paused and stared down at her hands, so like her *maman's* artistic ones.

Was her own inability to be happy for long in any one place simply in her genes? Inescapable? Fated?

"Brigitte," Lucas's voice was husky, his green eyes soft as moss. "You don't have to--"

She held up one hand. Something about Lucas's warm presence made her feel secure. He'd never use this against her.

"Sorry to ramble that way but let me get to the point. So, one time, we were staying in these rooms in a terrible neighborhood, just outside of Marseille. They weren't much-- upstairs from a small café. My mother went out with one of her boyfriends and left me at home."

"How old were you?" Lucas's brows drew together.

She blew out a breath. "I was eleven. I was used to being by myself. Taking care of myself. Anyway, I was alone, and it was very late, and the electricity went out in the neighborhood. It was pitch black inside and out. I've never liked the dark but now it was worse somehow knowing I couldn't turn on the light.

"Apparently the power had gone out in the area and some looters were busting out the windows in the shops and the bar downstairs. It was so loud. Then someone started banging on the door."

Suddenly, he was beside her, and clasped her hands with his large, warm ones. "Brigitte, this is terrible. I'm so sorry. I take it that wasn't your mother?"

She bit her lip. "*Non,* she didn't come back until morning. I didn't know what to do, so I wedged myself behind the ancient armoire. It was tiny and cramped and I was there for hours. These thieves broke down the door and ransacked our place but luckily they didn't discover me.

"I was there until she returned in the morning, like nothing at all had happened. And now, I cannot be in small dark places."

He wrapped his hard, muscular arms around her and rested his chin on the top of her head. "That's horrible. Parents are supposed to protect their children, not expose them to danger. What was she thinking leaving a little girl alone like that? What if those criminals had found you?"

A strange sense of comfort filled her as she rested her cheek against his solid chest. He smelled of soap and man and a hint of pine. Nobody had ever held her with this type of tenderness. She allowed herself another moment before shifting back.

"They didn't. And I think she did the best she could, but she wasn't really equipped to raise a child. But ever since that night, I've hated feeling boxed in and when the Escape Room walls narrowed and the gate dropped, it sent me back."

His eyes gleamed with compassion. "I bet. So how did you handle the metro in Paris and New York's subways? I hate going underground and I've really got no particular reason."

Her lips twitched. "I don't like it either. And I hadn't liked it even before that night in Marseille. I always walked or took a taxi."

The oven alarm dinged. Just in time. How had she shared so much with him?

She rose and hurried over to the kitchen. "We should eat and then it's your turn to confess all to me."

He followed her and took two gray stoneware plates from one of the cabinets. "Brigitte, I know that wasn't easy to tell me, and I'll make sure you never get stuck anywhere like that, okay?"

Warmth filled her. How was this man so sweet and so non-judgmental? His protective streak touched her heart.

"Well if we ever go to an Escape Room again, I'll make sure to learn more about the actual experience." She winked, seeking to lighten the mood.

"Good idea. Do you want another beer or something else to drink?"

"I'll have one more. It will complement the frittata." She cut a generous slice for Lucas and a narrow sliver for herself. The man was twice her size.

He grabbed two more bottles, they sat at the kitchen island, and ate in companionable silence.

"Okay, it's your turn. Shall we go back to the couch?" Helping him with what had happened earlier was why she'd come over. And she'd keep telling herself that.

CHAPTER 13

*L*ucas removed his glasses and massaged the bridge of his nose. Now he had more insight into why she'd passed out in the dark tunnel, and how her mom had shaped her lifestyle. No surprise she didn't know how to set down roots--because she'd never had any.

He tucked away her revelations to ponder later. What would make her want to stay? And why did he want her to stay so badly?

"Your turn in the hot seat." Her smile was mischievous, and her full lips were bare and tempting as hell.

His throat tightened--she was so damn beautiful. Tonight was the most casual he'd ever seen her--dressed in a pair of black leggings and a slim striped tunic. No Southern California athleisure style for her.

He took a moment to put his glasses on--he'd promised to share his sad little story and he didn't renege on his word. "Are you sure you want to hear this?"

"*Oui.* Now stop stalling and just tell me." Her slate-blue eyes narrowed, and she wagged a finger at him.

He inhaled a steadying breath. "So this happened a really long time ago, at the end of eighth grade."

"Your school system is different than what I grew up with. Were you eleven? A teenager?"

"I was thirteen and believe me when I tell you I was a really awkward kid." Talk about understatement.

She didn't respond but simply waved her hand for him to continue.

"So I was skinny, like painfully skinny. And pasty with freckles and this damn red hair. My eyes were terrible, basically legally blind, and back then, the choice of glasses was pathetic. Let's just say they looked more like goggles. If you ever saw that *Napoleon Dynamite* movie, that was me."

She giggled. "I believe you exaggerate. I cannot imagine you skinny, but I can picture the glasses."

His lips twitched. "I bet you can. In addition to being the goofiest looking kid, I was also really good at math. So I was the perfect target for the popular kids to bully."

"Oh, Lucas."

"Yeah, at least those were the days when nobody had smartphones yet. So there's that. Anyway, Jason was the ringleader of this group of boys who used to wait for me after school, shove me around, occasionally beat me up." His jaw tightened recalling every one of those little dickheads.

Brigitte's pale brow furrowed. "Couldn't someone at the school have stopped it?"

"Oh, my mom talked to the Principal a few times but usually it would only make it worse. They would wait for me off school grounds. Anyway, that was just how it was. But the incident that really made me realize I had a temper was a little different."

"Okay."

His mind rewound to that day. "It was the week before

finals and two things went down. I'd really wanted to play football over the summer and maybe even in high school. But Jason and his little cronies threatened me and told me no way would they let me play on their team."

"Little shits," Brigitte muttered, her dark brows drawn together.

"Yeah, they cornered me one day before I could approach the coach. They said they didn't like me, nobody would ever like me, and there was no way they would let me play on "their" team.

"I told them to go to hell and figured I'd sign up anyway. What could they do? But then the next day, Jason approached me at school and was acting all nice. He said he'd make me a deal. If I let him and his buddies cheat off me on the final math exam––because shocker, they all had shitty grades–– they would allow me to be on the team."

Brigitte snorted. "Seriously?"

"Seriously. Basically, if I didn't help them pass the final exam, not only would they not 'allow' me to be on the football team, they threatened to steal my dog and drop him off in the wilderness somewhere."

Brigitte smacked one hand on the couch. "Steal your dog? What kind of people would threaten your pet?"

"Oh, you'd be surprised. Well, I could handle the physical crap, I was young, and it was just how it was. But when they brought Harley into it, I was done. No way in hell was I putting up with them for one more day. So I used my brains and beat them at their own game."

She rubbed her hands together, her eyes gleaming. "Tell me. Tell me how you beat them."

He laughed at her enthusiasm. "I pretended to play along. Since I had the class first period and they had it later in the day, I told him I'd write down the answers and have it inside my calculator case. I mentioned I wouldn't give him every answer, just enough to pass. If those idiots suddenly got 100% on a math test, the teacher would know something was up.

"Yeah, he even said if I pulled it off, he'd make sure I got to play once in a while, at least in the scrimmages. The little prick." He rolled his eyes.

She scooted closer, a hint of her citrusy floral scent washing over him. "And so?"

"So, I wrote down all wrong answers for them and left the toughest questions blank because I knew they'd never figure them out. Regardless, even with what I'd given them, the highest they could score would be a D."

Brigitte's shoulders rocked with laughter. "That's fantastic. And did they all fail?"

He held up a hand. "That's not all. At the end of the day, I asked the math teacher to meet with me and the Principal. I told them what happened and that I'd given them incorrect responses. I gave them the cheat sheet and told them to check who had those answers on their tests. I also told them of the threats to Harley."

"Weren't you worried what they would do when they found out it was you?"

He grinned. "That's the brilliant thing. They never found out. The math teacher called them all for cheating and they got suspended. To protect me, the teacher included me in the group with the wrong answers but since I was usually a straight-A student, I just got a warning."

Approval gleamed in her eyes. "That's fantastic. And was that the end of it? Did you play football?"

He shook his head. "I decided it wasn't worth it. I'd gotten my revenge. Besides, I was too damn weak and skinny. I started lifting weights and ended up joining a boxing gym and learned to spar. In the Fall when they tried to give me crap, I was able to fight back."

She pressed one hand to her heart. "That's amazing. I wonder where those terrible boys are now?"

Lucas smirked. "No clue, except I'm pretty certain one of them lives in his mom's basement."

"Good. Now I have to ask. When did you get so…" She bit her plump lower lip and damn if her cheeks didn't pinken.

"So?" He wanted to hear her say it--sue him.

"Well, you're not skinny anymore. When did you become so big? I mean I saw you on the rugby field." She smoothed a strand of hair away from her face but kept her gaze down.

He grinned internally--Brigitte thought he was big. And was Ms. Confident Parisian acting coy?

He shrugged. "I had a growth spurt when I was sixteen, shot up to 6'2 and I kept boxing and lifting weights. I ended up playing football Senior year and that led to a rugby league in college, and I loved it."

"Hmm…"

Heat flashed through him at that moan. It was the sound she made when they'd kissed. When she'd been so responsive. So passionate. So fucking perfect. He sprang off the couch and sprinted to the kitchen.

Putting some distance between them. Needing some distance between them. Because she knocked him off-balance. He'd been attracted to her the moment he met her and with each passing day, that attraction deepened.

When he was with her, his logical thinking flew right out the window and instinct took over. And right now his instincts were to toss her over his shoulder and carry her to his bed.

Yeah, so the kitchen island was a mere defensive move. She'd come over tonight to check on him. To be a friend.

She'd trusted him enough to confide in him. And he'd done the same.

Intimate. The whole night was really intimate. So although he wanted her more than he'd ever wanted any woman, his analytical brain was calculating the risks.

The risks of him kissing her. Either way, if she rejected him, things would be awkward between them at work. Cost benefit ratio was precarious.

But even more dangerous? What if she wanted him as much as he wanted her? The way she was looking at him, her eyes heavy-lidded, her lips parted, her cheeks flushed? What if they spent the night together? What if he scared her away and she took off somewhere across the world?

She'd probably recover but based on his calculations, he might not. Brigitte was a dream woman, an incredible, brilliant, sexy, independent woman who might be able to be more casual about it all than he could. He'd be a fool to invest his emotions.

Because he couldn't kid himself. He was falling for Brigitte Thibault and that was one huge mark in the deficit column. Sleeping with her might send him tumbling into love from this infatuation. Neither of them were looking for anything serious.

And she'd made it clear already that she was a flight risk. His heart pounded.

"Lucas?"

Brigitte had joined him in the kitchen, and he hadn't even noticed he'd been so lost in his thoughts. He gazed down at her, and something tugged in his chest. Fuck, he was in trouble.

"Sorry about that." He forced a smile. "So, are we good?"

Keep it about their discussion, not their chemistry that thickened the air between them. Politely get her the hell out of the apartment before he did something they'd both regret.

"Thank you for listening to my story and for sharing yours." She paused and licked her lips.

His dick went hard. Was she trying to kill him? He retreated a step and nodded.

"We promised each other we'd keep our stories secret. Shall we seal the deal with a kiss?" Her warm floral scent surrounded him now she was so close. The heat from her skin, the flare of her pupils, the rise and fall of her chest signaled she was feeling something, too.

"A kiss?" Was that his voice, squeaky as it had been before he went through puberty?

Her lips curved upward, and she stepped closer, pressed one hand against his chest. "I know you Americans like to shake on a deal but we French prefer a kiss."

What could he do when she put it like that? She was so comfortable, so confident. He couldn't say no.

"Uh-huh." Yeah, words were not his friend right now.

She wound her arms around his neck and lifted her bare perfect lips. "Well?"

His control snapped and he cupped the back of her head in one hand, holding her in place. He captured her mouth, diving into her sweetness. When she moaned, he yanked her closer, one hand sliding down to her perfect ass. She arched her spine and melted against him. He coaxed her lips apart, their tongues tangling, dancing, sparring. Some primal emotion rose inside him––a stab of possessiveness. *Mine.*

He lifted his head and sucked in a harsh breath. "Brigitte, tell me you want me."

She pressed her palm against his aching erection and lightly squeezed. "Yes. I want you. Now."

He groaned and slanted his mouth against hers again. He scooped her up and she wrapped her legs around his waist. Without breaking their kiss, he carried her into his bedroom and dropped her on the bed. She propped herself up on her elbows and gazed at him, her eyes blazing. She beckoned for him to join her.

This might not be his most logical move, but right now, he was trusting his gut. And it told him being with Brigitte was right...at least tonight.

CHAPTER 14

*L*ucas yanked off his t-shirt with one hand and tossed it aside. He stood before her looking like Michelangelo had sculpted him as a tribute to male beauty. She swallowed, her throat parched, and simply stared. His body was a work of art, from his broad shoulders, square pecs, and ridged abs which narrowed down to those carved V-shaped grooves that disappeared into the low-slung sweats which were now her favorite item of clothing.

The soft fabric emphasized just how hard he was, the ridge of his impressive cock straining to be free. He looked delicious and an overwhelming urge to taste him flooded through her.

She shifted forward until she was on the edge of the bed. He was frozen in place, his eyes blazing behind his glasses.

She reached up and stroked one hand along his washboard abs, which were impossibly hard. He sucked in a breath but didn't move. She ran one finger along the waistband of his sweatpants and paused when she reached the drawstring. She tugged it open, impatient now.

When he sprang free, she gasped and for a moment could

only stare. He was perfect here, too. Huge, smooth, and hard as steel. Keeping her gaze locked with his, she wrapped one hand around him, her fingers barely able to connect. His chest rumbled as he stared down at her.

"Brigitte," he rasped.

A swell of feminine power surged through her. Tonight, she and Lucas were woman and man, not employee and boss or even friends. Tonight, she wanted to take control, to give him pleasure. His barely leashed arousal spurred her on.

Taking her sweet time, she lowered her head, trailed kisses along those sexy grooves on the front of his hips and nibbled her way across and pressed a light kiss on his cock. She teased him with her tongue before she opened and took him in one quick move, until he hit the back of her throat. He tasted of soap and salt and a hint of musk--delicious.

His breath hissed out and his hips jerked forward. He fisted a hand into her hair, holding her in place. Not so firmly that she couldn't control the pace but with a strength that had heat blossoming low in her belly. She stroked her hands along his hips and dug her short nails into his high, muscular butt.

"Brigitte, if you don't stop I'll lose it right here." She gave another leisurely lick before she reluctantly released him, and he looked down at her. "Lift your arms up."

She complied, and he tugged her top off and tossed it aside. She hadn't worn a bra--frankly she'd never needed one because her breasts weren't large enough to require any extra support.

"Fuck, you are so beautiful." He stepped out of his sweatpants and lowered one knee to the bed beside her. "I want to see all of you."

The hint of authority in his voice had her melting from the inside out. Together, they removed her leggings and moved up onto the bed. He propped himself on one elbow and looked at her, desire burning in his deep green eyes.

He stroked her collarbones with long, blunt fingers, the pads surprisingly rough for a man who worked with numbers. But Lucas was nothing like what she'd expected.

Taking his time, he circled one nipple with his thumb, her nipples pebbled, and a flash of heat shot straight to her center.

"So responsive. So perfect." He lowered his head and raked his teeth across her breast and his mouth closed over her, his tongue stroking and teasing.

She moaned his name and arched into his touch, goose-bumps erupting along her skin, liquid heat sparking through her. She thrust her fingers into his thick, silky hair.

He shifted his attention to her other breast and trailed those strong hands down her ribcage, across the planes of her stomach, and moved lower. He slid one hand between her legs, and thrust one thick finger inside her, then a second. "You're so wet, so hot." He bit lightly on her nipple, sending shockwaves of sensation through her.

He found an intoxicating rhythm and when he circled her clit with his thumb, she rocked against his hand. Sensation pulsated through her and when he lifted his head and captured her mouth, she came apart in shimmering waves.

She bowed up, lost in sensation. All she knew was she wanted more. She wanted all of him.

"Lucas, I want you inside me now, please." She raked her fingernails down his back. "Protection. Please tell me you have some close by."

His lips curved against her damp skin. "So impatient. I need to taste you first."

Before she could protest, he slid down her body, leaving a trail of fire with his lips, his tongue, before positioning his wide shoulders between her thighs.

He paused, his gaze focused on her center. "So perfect here, soft and pink, just like I imagined."

"Mmm, you imagined?" He'd been fantasizing about her, too?

He gave a harsh laugh. "You have no idea."

Slowly, he lowered his head and pressed a soft kiss on her center. Her hips rocked up, but he gripped her thighs, spread her wider, and held her in place. He licked her in one long stroke, then dove in like she was the most delicious treat he'd ever sampled.

His talented tongue teased and stroked, setting her aflame. Unable to move, she received the pleasure he gave and when he added two fingers inside her and found that magical spot, unbelievably tremors started pulsing through her again, every nerve ending sparking and burning.

This time she couldn't hold back the scream as the orgasm crashed through her. Again. He held her until the waves subsided and kissed his way back up her shaking, satisfied body. When he captured her mouth, she tasted herself on his lips, felt the intense connection between them.

"You okay?" He murmured.

"Mmm…okay is not the word I would use. What are you doing to me?" She stroked her fingers along his powerful shoulders.

He lifted his head and brushed her damp hair away from her face. "Making you feel good and we're just getting started. I need to be inside you."

Her heart hammered in her chest, her breath coming in short bursts. "Yes." Anticipation danced along her skin.

He rolled to the side and grabbed a condom from the bedside table. He shifted back and gazed down at her, his eyes hooded. "You are the most beautiful woman I've ever seen."

She exhaled a shaky breath. "Well, we're even because

you're the most beautiful man I've ever seen. Now fuck me before I lose my mind."

Without breaking their gaze, he ripped open the foil packet and rolled the condom over his length. He dropped down to his powerful forearms and positioned himself between her thighs. He managed to keep the bulk of his weight from crushing her and took her mouth in a hot possessive kiss.

She stroked her hands down his back and caught his round, muscular ass in her hands. Urging him on. Desperate for him to fill her.

He trailed his lips along her jawline, and lightly bit the tender spot on the side of her neck. He entered her slowly, inch by inch, giving her time to adjust to his considerable size. Her breath released on a long moan--he was huge. Incredibly deep inside her, filling her completely.

He held himself still and lifted his head. "Are you okay? Do you need a minute?"

"I've never been more full but I'm more than okay. You feel incredible." *Like you were made for me.*

He growled low in his throat. "You feel like heaven, so hot, so tight."

He began to move in slow powerful strokes, and she wrapped her legs around his back, tilting her hips up so he hit her at the perfect angle. They found a natural rhythm, and he slid one hand beneath her hips, each stroke deeper, harder, more intense. Their skin grew slick with sweat, the only sound in his bedroom their pants, their bodies moving together, and whispered words of pleasure.

He reached down and stroked her where they were connected. Her back bowed up and her legs tightened around him.

Her body began quaking again--could she really be coming apart a third time--and tremors flooded through her. "Lucas," she screamed his name and rocked against him.

"Yes," he groaned, and his hips slammed against hers as he followed her over the edge.

For a minute, he collapsed on top of her before pushing up to one powerful forearm. "Did I hurt you?" His emerald eyes searched hers.

Her lips curved upward. "Oh no, you pleased me very much."

His eyes drifted shut, his hair flopped over his forehead, and he looked shy for a moment.

She laughed. "After that, you're feeling bashful? And when did you take off your glasses?" Their time together in the bedroom was one sensual blur.

His lips twitched. "Let's just say they would've gotten in the way a little while ago."

He pressed a soft kiss against her lips. "Let me take care of the condom." He withdrew and headed to the ensuite bathroom.

She enjoyed the play of the light on his sinewy muscles and gorgeous body. She arched up and stretched like a cat, enjoying the heaviness in her limbs. Satisfaction saturated every cell of her body. Had she ever felt so relaxed and satiated? She couldn't remember.

Lucas returned and together they slid beneath the smooth sheets.

He shifted onto his side, wrapped his arms around her, and pulled her against his hard body. "You'll stay with me tonight."

Usually, she never spent the night. Easier to leave and avoid the intimacy of breakfast or expectations of spending the day together. But with Lucas, falling asleep in the warm circle of his arms felt natural. Felt right.

Plenty of time to worry about that tomorrow.

*L*ucas buried his face into Brigitte's soft hair and inhaled her sweet fragrance. He slid his hand up her warm silky skin and captured one sensitive breast. Holy hell, waking up with her in his arms was heaven.

She moaned, her nipples tightened into stiff peaks, and she arched the curve of her ass against him. He slid his hand down and cupped her, sliding one finger into her wet heat.

"You're ready for me," he rasped against the sweet curve of her neck.

She angled her head back. "I am but I'm a little tender."

His gut tightened. Damn it, he knew he'd been too rough with her. "I'm sorry." He started to retreat.

She wrapped her slender fingers around his wrist, holding him still. "Oh, don't apologize. I loved every minute. I was going to suggest we go into the shower."

His dick twitched at her suggestion. Her accent somehow made everything she said even sexier. Hell, she could read the contractor's punch list and make it sound like some erotic adventure.

"I love the way you think." He caught her around the

waist, rolled them to the side, and scooped her up in his arms.

She looped her arms around his neck and pressed an open-mouthed kiss on his throat. "Let me grab another condom."

He paused and she leaned down and picked up a foil packet from the pile they'd dropped there in the middle of the night. Yeah, they'd been busy. Best night of his life.

He fisted his hand in her hair, tugged her head back, and kissed her. She moaned and melted against him, every inch of her driving him mad. He strode to the bathroom, whipped the glass shower door open with one hand and flipped on the faucet. Steam filled the room, and he carried her into the shower.

He pivoted without breaking the kiss, pressed her back against the smooth tiles, and adjusted her legs around his waist. She rocked her hips against him and thrust her fingers into his hair. He was ready to enter her in one stroke, but a moment of sanity hit him, and he remembered she'd admitted she was sore. They'd had three incredible sessions over the course of the night, and he hadn't been gentle.

Not that she'd wanted gentle. He gritted his teeth. Much as he wanted to take her hard against the wall, he didn't want to hurt her. He kept kissing her but released her legs and groaned at the feel of her sliding down his body.

"*Non*, what are you doing? I want you to fuck me against the wall." She protested and dug her fingers into his scalp.

"Woman, you're going to kill me. Let me take care of you first."

She pouted when he reached for the bath gel and rubbed it between his hands. He started at her narrow shoulders, traveled across her delicate collarbones, and stroked down her sleek gorgeous body. He nudged her legs apart with one knee and massaged the gel on her most sensitive spots.

She moaned and her head dropped back against the wall, her dark lashes fanned out on her cheekbones. For a moment, he could only stare. She was the hottest vision he'd ever seen. He played and teased her with his fingers, sliding one inside her, then two. When he added a third, she cried out his name and he almost exploded on the spot.

He dropped to his knees, slid his hand under one long thigh and placed it over his shoulder, holding her in place. He gazed up. "You're going to come in my mouth and then I'm going to take you against this wall."

"Lucas, yes," she breathed his name.

He lowered his head and dove into her sweetness, his blood flaming, his senses immersed in the taste of her, the feel of her leg trembling on his shoulder, and her cries urging him on. Her hips bucked against him, and she began coming apart for him. He gripped her hips and kept up his assault until the waves pulsing through her stopped and she went still.

"Lucas, that was amazing. Please come up here. I want you inside me."

He didn't need to be asked twice. He surged to his feet, ripped open the foil packet he'd tossed onto the shower shelf, and sheathed himself.

Her lips curved upward; her eyes hooded. He slanted his mouth across hers and their tongues danced and twirled in a slow sensual rhythm. She pressed up onto her toes and lifted one leg up. He caught her hips, and she wrapped her legs around his waist again. She braced her hands on his shoulders, lightly digging her nails into his skin.

He filled her in one stroke and her tight heat gripped him like a fist and he groaned. "Fuck, you feel incredible."

"Mmm-hmm, I love the way you fill me up." She tugged his head down and kissed him, her breath sweet and hot.

He began taking her in long, sure strokes, the shower wall

holding her in place. He dropped his forehead against the tile and buried himself in her. Her hands slid down to his ass and pulled him closer, urging him on.

His lower back began to burn and tingle, signaling he was close. He adjusted the angle of his hips, desperate to give her another orgasm before he let go.

"Yes, right there. More, more, more. I'm so close. Come with me."

"I'm coming," he cried and dropped his head to the tender spot where her neck and shoulder met. His climax slammed through him, his mind blanked, and his knees went weak.

For a few moments, only the spray of the shower and their ragged breathing filled the silence. He lifted his head, released her legs, and braced his hands against the tiles working to find his equilibrium. *Holy hell.*

She gazed up at him, her eyes blazing a deeper shade of blue, her lips parted. "Well, I'm not sure if I'll be able to walk today but I officially don't care."

He barked out a laugh. "Same. Maybe we should just go back to bed, but you'll have to walk this time. I don't think I have any strength left to carry you."

She grinned, all mischievous sparkling eyes and gleaming white teeth. "I think the bed is where this all started so perhaps now it's time to actually clean up. We have to go to Paramount today, remember?"

He groaned. "Oh yeah. And I think that's where all this really started."

And oh shit, yeah, now they had to go to work. What now? Did they pretend like nothing had happened and it was business as usual? Or was this the beginning of something new? He retreated a step, closed his eyes, and scrubbed his hands through his hair. He'd promised himself he wouldn't succumb to temptation and here he was.

"Lucas," she said, her voice quiet. "Don't freak out, okay. This doesn't change anything."

He opened his eyes and studied her now serious expression. "Doesn't change anything?" What the hell?

She reached out and brushed her fingers along his jaw. "Last night was incredible. This morning is incredible but what I mean is we're still working together. We don't need to do anything. And we keep this between ourselves."

On that he agreed. And not just because of the bet. He didn't give a crap about that now. But if his friends knew they'd slept together, there would be questions. And now that they were all cozily in love and planning on marriage, they wanted him to be on the same page.

Maybe they could juggle it all, but he couldn't. Maybe if he was just the CFO still, he could handle a relationship, or a friends with benefits or whatever the hell else with Brigitte. Because he could be a CFO in his sleep. Numbers were his happy place and his confidence in that arena was unmatched.

But truth be told, he was treading water trying to keep up with everything opening a new luxury boutique hotel entailed. He didn't have an extra minute to devote to dating or a relationship or hell, even a friends with benefits scenario. Not if he wasn't going to let his friends down. Logic dictated she was right so why did his chest ache?

Unsure of how to respond, he grabbed some shower gel, and lifted his face into the shower spray, willing the water to rinse away the new host of trouble he'd created by sleeping with Brigitte. He took care of the condom with one hand.

She stroked one hand down his back. "Lucas? Are we okay?"

He nodded. "Yeah, got it." He rinsed off. "I'll make some coffee and let you finish in here."

Maybe he was being abrupt but right now, he needed a couple minutes to pull it together. It's not like he hadn't had casual hook-ups before, but Brigitte was not just any woman. He'd started out with a crush on her and now...now it was complicated. She was best friends with Charlie--his best friend's wife--which meant she would be in his life forever. Not awkward at all.

Well, unless she bailed and took off to the other side of the world. She'd made it clear she wasn't the type to plant roots. Who could blame her for not settling in one place after her childhood? And she had made it crystal clear she was a mature woman who valued her freedom.

Yeah, he just needed a little time alone to compartmentalize it all. Tuck away these unfamiliar possessive feelings she evoked in him deep into the vault. Keep his like and admiration for her on the surface. He'd be her boss, her friend from a distance, and stay away from anything deeper.

Safer that way for his equilibrium.

Safer for his career.

And safer for his heart.

BRIGITTE COLLECTED last night's clothes from various spots around Lucas's bedroom. She winced as she slid on her leggings--she hadn't been joking about being tender. And after what just happened in the shower? She'd be walking like one of those Western rodeo queens she'd seen on television.

Not that she regretted last night. But last night she'd shared things about her difficult upbringing that only Charlie knew. She'd felt safe with him. Loved his compassion, his protectiveness, his concern.

And he'd confided personal things as well. They'd shared intimate details of their lives, not just chemistry and that was new. But entangling work and pleasure was dangerous, and work had to remain the priority.

Had that been a flash of hurt in his eyes when she'd said nothing had changed? What did he expect? She shook her head. If she could compartmentalize their physical attraction, certainly he could, too.

But their best friends were married. *Merde.* She bit her lip. Charlie.

Charlie had asked her to help Lucas out at work and the man needed help opening the hotel, not a secret lover.

Although part of her whispered that all her rationalizations justified them hooking up and keeping work and pleasure separate, right? Why couldn't they have a discreet fling? Their chemistry was off the charts. If she was honest with herself, she'd have to acknowledge that Lucas Sutton was the best lover she'd ever had.

Not just his carved from marble body and his considerable skills. But he was so attuned to her. So focused on pleasing her but at the same time taking charge—somehow sensitive and commanding. The buttoned up accountant was growly and demanding in bed and she loved every minute of it.

Smoothing down her wrinkled tunic, she followed the scent of coffee brewing and joined Lucas in the kitchen.

His back was to her, and he wore a pale blue dress shirt, tailored to fit his broad shoulders and taper to his narrow waist. His slim charcoal trousers displayed his ass to perfection. The man knew how to dress and damned if that wasn't attractive.

Not that she hadn't appreciated him shirtless in a pair of sweatpants, and naked in bed but there was something about a sharply dressed man that turned her on. Something tightened in her chest, and she tamped it down.

No time to become sentimental or sappy. Lucas was a nice man who was a great lover. That was it.

She'd keep it light. "Look at you ready to slay Beverly Hills and here I am in last night's clothes."

He turned with a mug of steaming coffee and handed it to her. "You look beautiful in anything you put on."

"You're too kind. Is it okay if I return the mug to you later? I've got an appointment in an hour and need to hurry if I'm going to make it in time."

He nodded. "Of course, I need to get into the office now, too." His tone was even, and he was perfectly polite.

Quite the contrast to thirty minutes ago in the shower. Heat crept up the back of her neck and she sipped of her coffee. Well, this was…awkward. It would all be fine once they got to Paramount.

Hopefully.

CHAPTER 16

rigitte collapsed onto a wrought iron bench, beside an enormous jacaranda tree. She was exhausted physically, mentally, and emotionally. Last night had been more intimate than anything she'd experienced before--she couldn't fit Lucas into the category of casual hook-up or friends with benefits. And they hadn't slept much.

The meeting with the Gagosian Gallery curator had gone well and they'd agreed upon some exclusive showings and passes for Paramount guests. Because the gallery rotated international artists and exhibits throughout the year, hotel guests who visited frequently always had something new to see.

Right now? She'd indulge in a few minutes basking in the perfect Southern California weather. The kiss of the crisp late morning breeze and the warmth of the sun soothed her jangled nerves. Her eyes drifted closed behind her dark sunglasses. Just for a few minutes before she mainlined another double espresso.

Flashbacks from last night played like a movie montage

behind her eyelids. Lucas's intense emerald gaze, his pure physical strength, and his focus on giving her pleasure sparked a curl of heat down her spine. The compassion he'd expressed when she'd shared her childhood story and the flash of pain he'd revealed when he shared his own. Yes, she had intimacy issues but with Lucas, she felt secure. Safe.

Her phone buzzed and Charlie's name appeared. She pressed one hand to her roiling belly––surely a result of the excessive caffeine and not anxiety about last night.

"Hi Charlie, *quoi de neuf?*"

"I love how you make me practice my teeny bit of French. Nothing's new around here but I was checking in to see what's going on there? Have you had to save the day for Lucas again?"

Annoyance flared up her spine. "Lucas isn't a project. He's a very capable, intelligent man. And no, he hasn't needed any help."

"Whoa, don't bite my head off. I was just asking."

Brigitte huffed out a breath. "Well, the scene with Dagmar was rough but in Lucas's defense, ninety percent of the population can't handle that woman. The only reason they put up with her drama is because her eye is so good."

"Brigitte, I––"

"*Non*, listen to me. You should have seen him handle this total criminal from the permit place, he was masterful. I'm uncomfortable about the entire thing. Like I'm going behind his back or something." Would the warmth in his expressive green eyes cool if he found out?

The line went dead.

"Charlie? Are you still there?"

Charlie cleared her throat. "I'm here but I'm in a bit of a shock."

"Shock?"

"Umm, yes. I'm not used to you defending somebody like

this. It's not like you're being dishonest. You're just making sure you're there to lend a helping hand if he needs it."

"Well, I would do that with anyone. Now that I'm getting to know him better it feels disrespectful. And he deserves to be respected." She impatiently brushed a strand of hair that the breeze kept whipping across her cheek.

"Okaaaaay. Is there something you're not telling me?"

"What do you mean?" *Uh-oh.*

"Come on, Brigitte. You're my best friend. You're acting strange. I saw the sparks between you two when I was up there for the weekend."

She studied her fingernails. It was time for a manicure. "We've become friends, that's all. I like Lucas. And I respect him. He doesn't need to have me spying on him."

Charlie sputtered. "You are not spying on him, for god's sake. It's not like you're giving reports on him or even telling me if you did need to help him with the permits. I think you *like him*, like him. Did you two hook up?"

Brigitte's breath lodged in her throat. Deflect, deflect, deflect. She'd never lied to her best friend, and she refused to start now. They didn't keep secrets from each other. But she and Lucas had agreed to keep last night private.

She'd been the one to suggest they not tell anyone.

It wasn't just her and Charlie anymore. Charlie and Ryan had that married couple-we-keep-no-secrets-vibe. And she wouldn't want to put Charlie in the position to have to hide something from her husband.

So perhaps she could divert her best friend's attention without actually telling a lie.

"Look, I like him and yes, I do find him attractive. I saw him playing rugby and let me tell you, he's built like a gladiator. But I've also gotten to know him better and while he might be more reserved with people than you or me, he can handle difficult people. Okay?"

"Hmm, okay. I'll let it be. But yes, he's got the ultimate hot professor vibe going on. And you know I respect him very much. So…"

"So?"

"I trust your judgment. We have a lot riding on Paramount's success, not just for the hotel but for the whole chain. So, if you can keep your eyes and ears open and step in if needed, I'd feel a lot better."

She sighed. "Charlie, it will be. And of course if I will do everything I can to ensure Paramount is incredible. Anyway, what else is going on?"

"Okay, great. Oh, I wanted to give you a head's up. Dave Golden is going to start tomorrow. Originally he was slated for next week, but his schedule shifted. Having Sales and Marketing onsite will alleviate some pressure off Lucas."

"Good. That way you aren't juggling all the Sales and Marketing for Pacific Jewel Inn, overseeing all the Directors, and working on Paramount, too." Charlie was a workaholic.

"It helps. And Jon will be up there with you all soon, in the job you should be doing now."

Brigitte grimaced. "Enough with the Assistant G.M. stuff. I told you I don't want that role, okay?"

"Fine. As long as you stay. Are you happy living in Beverly Hills so far? Is it starting to feel like home yet?"

Brigitte surveyed the gorgeous scenery around her, the manicured trees, powder blue sky, and elegant buildings. It was pretty but was it home? What if the novelty wore off and she became bored, like she had everywhere other place she'd lived?

"So far, I like it here. But I did think we'd see each other more." A wave of restlessness drifted through her.

"We will, I promise. Once Paramount opens, we'll be able to see each other more regularly. I'm happy being only a few hour drive away from you instead of thousands of miles. And we'll be up for the Soft Launch party. I think that's a great way to build excitement."

"I like Lucas's idea as well. And on that note, there's a lot to do before December 10th. I should get going. Love you."

"Love you, too."

Brigitte dropped her phone into her scarlet satchel and rose to her feet. Okay, although she hadn't technically lied to Charlie, she prided herself with being authentic and honest. One day she'd share with Charlie about the hottest night of her life.

But for now, if Charlie or anyone else discovered they'd slept together, drama would ensue. She gave a sharp nod and started back to the hotel, intent on finding Lucas to ensure they were on the same page. Discuss it one more time.

Last night had been incredible, but it was only one night. One special, secret night.

After stopping for a double espresso, she paused in front of the entrance and admired the seven-story façade, which boasted beautiful architecture. The renovation stayed true to the original 1933 building, but the paint and stucco had been lovingly restored. She allowed herself to imagine what it would look like once they were open––elegant and bustling with well-dressed guests, eager to reach their fabulous rooms.

"It's going to be the best hotel in Beverly Hills." A deep voice said beside her.

She turned and a tall man with chestnut hair and soft brown eyes grinned down at her.

"Yes, that's exactly what Paramount will be. Thank you for noticing."

"Well, it's my job. I'm Dave Golden, the Director of Sales and Marketing for the hotel."

She returned his smile. "I'm Brigitte Thibault, the Concierge. Nice to meet you. Lucas will be thrilled to see you. Pre-launch is quite busy, and we need all the help we can get."

"I don't officially start until tomorrow, but I couldn't resist coming by to see the progress. You available to show me around?"

"I'm afraid not but I'll take you to Lucas's office. But be careful, he may put you to work." She reached for the door, but he was already opening it.

He winked and waved her through the entrance. "After you. Lucas has always been a hard worker, no surprise there. I can't wait to see him. It's been years since we were in school together."

Together they traversed the bustling lobby aka storage depot, which was an explosion of supplies and boxes, covering the makeshift plywood flooring. They waved and said hello to a few of the sub-contractors busy at work. Fortunately, the black and white tile had arrived from Italy this week and was scheduled to be installed. Already, the walls had been painted alabaster, the ceilings were bright, and the crown moldings added elegance despite the mess.

"Wow, this is going to be incredible. I've seen some photos, but it just feels great in here, you know?"

Ah, Dave Golden understood the importance of ambiance. Of course he did––Ryan and Lucas wouldn't have hired him if he hadn't.

"Yes, I'm thrilled. Follow me to Lucas's office."

She knocked on his closed door and he called out "Come in.".

Lucas sat behind his large desk, a crease between his thick eyebrows. "Dave? Did I get the days wrong?"

Dave laughed and strode inside. "If you did, you've lost your touch. No, I start tomorrow but I couldn't resist stopping by. The beautiful Ms. Thibault was kind enough to bring me back."

Lucas's jaw tightened for a beat then he smoothed his expression and rose to meet Dave. "Good timing, I can put you to work right now."

Dave pulled Lucas in for one of those one-armed man hugs. "Great to see you. It's been too long. I'm so glad to be a part of the team."

Brigitte was sure Dave hadn't caught the flicker of annoyance on Lucas's face, but she had. Was he jealous? Not that he had any reason to be.

She studied the two men. Dave was tall, but a few inches shorter than Lucas. He had a lean, elegant frame, without Lucas's broad shoulders. He was handsome, outgoing, and polished--the kind of man she'd usually be attracted to, but she felt no spark of attraction.

Unlike the way her heart kicked against her ribs looking at Lucas's gladiator physique and quiet demeanor. Yes, they needed to make sure they were on the same page after last night but right now, some space was the best solution.

Brigitte cleared her throat. "Excuse me guys, I'm heading back to my office now."

Lucas caught her gaze, his eyes gleaming. "How did the gallery meeting go? Do you need anything?"

Another taste of you? "It was great, thanks. I'm fine for now."

"Great, that's great."

Dave glanced between the two of them, brows raised. "Everything's great around here, I guess?" He laughed.

Brigitte forced a casual smile. "It absolutely is, you'll see. Nice to meet you."

She pivoted to leave, the heat from Lucas's emerald eyes searing her back. She'd underestimated the impact seeing him again after this morning's shower would have on her. Time to pull herself together and be the professional boss babe she was reputed to be.

"Holy shit, she's gorgeous. What's her story? Is she single?" Dave whistled.

Lucas's spine stiffened. "Dude, you're here to work, not hit on the concierge."

Dave held up both hands. "Whoa, I'm not hitting on her, and I don't start until tomorrow. I'm just asking. There aren't any rules prohibiting dating, right?"

Lucas turned back toward his desk. Yeah, he needed to keep it together. No need for Dave to suspect he was crazy about Brigitte. Hell, he'd only admitted to himself how he was falling for her. But he sure wasn't going to sit around and encourage someone else to ask her out.

"Nope, no rules." Thank god. "Anyway, I'm glad to see you because this pre-launch is no joke and I need all the help I can get."

Dave studied him, his gaze assessing. "I wanted to just take a look around before I come in tomorrow. I'm still settling into my place. Does that work?"

"Of course. I'm about to hop onto another conference

call. You can sit in if you want, or you can explore on your own until I'm off in about forty-five."

"I've only got about half an hour, so if it's cool with you, I'll wander around. Where's my office?"

"Sure. Your office is two doors down the hall, on the left side. And then I'll see you tomorrow at 8:00? We can meet and then we've got a video conference with Charlie and Ryan at 9:00."

Dave waved as he strode out the door. "Deal, see you tomorrow."

"Hey, grab one of the hard hats from the lobby if you go upstairs. They've got some serious work happening up there."

Lucas sank back into his chair, clicked on his laptop and hit "Join" for his conference call. He was a few minutes early, so he whipped off his glasses and massaged the bridge of his nose. Right now his concentration was non-existent.

Because yeah, when Dave asked about Brigitte, a flash of jealousy hit him. She'd said nothing had changed but everything had changed. A casual one-night stand or the start of a friends with benefits or...? Damn it, just like he'd figured, mixing business and pleasure was complicated.

He replaced his glasses and managed to participate on the short budget and financing call. His comfort zone.

And now it was time to step out of that comfort zone and talk to Brigitte. He texted her and they agreed to meet in her office in twenty minutes. Time to get everything sorted and clarified because after this morning he needed boundaries.

When he reached her open doorway, he paused for a moment and simply stared. She stood at her window, talking on the phone. Her silky dark hair was in a low bun, and she wore a tailored white blouse and red slacks, which emphasized her subtle curves.

Her beauty stole his breath, especially after last night.

And after last night, his simple crush wasn't so simple any longer. Something tugged in his chest.

She turned, held up one slender hand, and gestured to the navy velvet chair facing her desk. He closed the door behind him and sat, biding his time until she finished her call. He tapped his fingers along his thigh and glanced around her office, so he'd stop ogling her.

Piles of books were strewn everywhere and if hadn't seen the top of her laptop lid, he wouldn't have found it beneath the mountain of stuff on her desk. The place looked like a library or stationery store had thrown up on it. What the hell?

"I see the horror on your face. You've caught me." Brigitte approached and rested a hip against the corner of her desk.

"Caught you?"

She shrugged and bit her lower lip between her small white teeth. "I'm not as tidy as you are."

"You mean this is how your desk always looks? I thought maybe someone broke in looking for something?" He bit the inside of his cheek to keep from cracking up.

She pressed her hand to her mouth, her shoulders shaking. "Very funny. Okay, confession time. I do have a system."

He gave up and laughed. "And what is the system?"

"I can find anything on my desk or in my drawers. Call it intuition?" She raised an eyebrow.

"Okay, prove it to me. Where's the portfolio on The Private Suite?"

"Oh, I know exactly where that is. Hold on." She pawed through the clutter on her desk, shoving one pile out of the way and digging into another.

"Tick-tock." He tapped his index finger on his watch.

"Hey, I'll find it. Give me a second." She pulled out a black folder with gold-foil lettering. "Aha, here it is."

He cracked up. "Okay, I don't have time to test out more

but bravo. I didn't know this was the way you, ahem, organized things." It was pretty cute.

Her smile faltered. "We've only known each other a short while. I'm sure there are many things we don't know about each other, right?"

He swallowed. Here was his opening. "Fair point. And that's part of why we need to talk now. To figure out how we move forward after…"

"After last night? *Oui*, you're right. And what are you suggesting we do?"

"I think we need to be on the same page. We need to do what makes the most sense." As if anything about the two of them together made sense.

"The most sense? So we're approaching it from the logical perspective, which I suppose shouldn't surprise me." Her voice rose and her accent deepened.

"Well, yeah, a logical perspective. We work together. The rest of the team has a bet running about us sleeping together, which we did. We've got a hectic pre-launch we both need to be focused on. We've got to be smart about this." If he didn't know better, he'd think she was pissed. How could she be angry with him when he was trying to act like a responsible adult?

She crossed her arms across her chest. "And by smart do you mean we pretend like it didn't happen? Or smart we tell everyone, so they stop harassing us about the bet?"

"This morning you said last night didn't change anything. That we should keep it between us. Last night was––" He ran his tongue around his teeth because, damn there were so many things he could say.

"Last night was amazing." Her voice was husky.

He lifted his gaze and caught a flicker of emotion in her eyes. "Last night was amazing. You're amazing but now we're back at work and I'm not sure what's the best path forward."

"Do you always have a plan? A "best path forward?""

He threw up his hands. "I try to have a plan. What's wrong with that? It's who I am. And so we have a few options. We can pretend like last night never happened. We can acknowledge that last night was mind-blowing, but it can't happen again or--?"

Brigitte pushed away from the desk and stalked to the window, her back to him. "We are very different, you and me. But I agree it's complicated. So, let's make it simple.

"We can agree last night was incredible, but it was one night. Moving forward we will return to being friends and colleagues. We're adults, like you said. *D'accord?*"

The tension in her shoulders revealed she wasn't as unaffected as she claimed. Hell, he'd been inside her hours ago, he recognized her body language better now.

And she was right. Now wasn't the time to dissect how far beyond a crush his feelings for her had progressed. Despite wanting to spend more time with her, to get to know her better, to spend another night or nights with her, he was a realist.

And the reality was he was over his head with her, and he was over his head with this damn job. He gripped his thighs and forced his breath to stay even.

If he pressured Brigitte to go public, to explore whether they could have a future together, she'd probably catch the first plane out of town.

If he looked too closely at what he really wanted for his career as opposed to what he was doing, he risked letting his best friends down. He'd committed to running Paramount and he couldn't quit. Not now.

"Lucas?" Brigitte turned, her pale oval face expressionless. "*D'accord* means okay."

"I know what it means. I think at this point, simple makes the most sense. And I think we keep it between us. But I don't want you think that last night wasn't special because it was."

"It was. Simple it is. And on that note, I have another meeting to prepare for."

A flicker of disappointment went through him. How contradictory could he be? Did he want her to fight for something different when he knew they couldn't have anything more? At least not yet? But she was nothing if not confident and unflappable and that was part of her appeal.

Regret filled him but he pushed to his feet. He stood, unsure if he should just walk out or hug her or what. "Of course. Me, too."

After a few uncomfortable moments, she waved a hand, picked up her phone, and returned to the large picture window.

Dismissed. Only time would tell if he could file away last night's memories and today's feelings. Paramount was his priority, and it was time to get back to work. With a tightness in his throat, he left. It would all work itself out, right?

CHAPTER 18

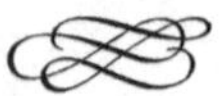

*M*id-November

Brigitte zipped up her black leather motorcycle jacket and adjusted her crimson cashmere scarf. Although the Southern California days were sunny and mild, the evenings grew quite cool. Maybe she was overdressing but after all those years in the Caribbean, she wasn't accustomed to fifty degree nights. Besides, tonight was the Rodeo Drive Holiday Lighting Celebration, and the red scarf felt festive.

The last few weeks had flown by in a whirlwind of meetings, planning, and all things pre-launch. Dave Golden had jumped into the fray straight away and was getting a lot accomplished. Except for weekly skeleton staff meetings, she had barely seen Lucas. On one hand, this was a positive because out of sight out of mind. But on the other hand, once the work frenzy slowed down and she returned to her condo alone, he filled her thoughts and her dreams. She missed him.

After their discussion about how to handle their hook up, she'd been feeling unsettled. She'd always had a restless nature but now, she was questioning some of her choices. Was she afraid of what would happen if she planted roots? Yes, she could have pushed Lucas, but fear had won out because what if he'd agreed to see her and these unfamiliar emotions deepened?

So maybe on some level, she'd wanted him to push to keep seeing her. He'd disappointed her when he had talked about logic and boundaries instead of feelings. The passionate man from the night before, the wild man from the rugby field, had been subsumed by the buttoned-up accountant. After she'd uncovered what was beneath the surface, somehow she'd wanted more.

The discussion had been necessary, and their decision was the safest move. But she'd never played it safe before so now, she'd focused one hundred percent on work and zero percent on fun. And she was getting cranky.

Sex with Lucas had been spectacular, and he'd reawakened her taste for it. Sure, she could have swiped right or however those dating apps worked but she hadn't wanted to meet someone new. She wanted Lucas.

Which was most inconvenient.

Dave Golden had been flirtatious but had gotten the hint when she placed him squarely in the friend zone. Since then, she'd enjoyed working with him. Tonight, Dave, Lucas, and she were attending the Rodeo Drive Holiday Lighting Celebration which was apparently a very big deal in Beverly Hills. There would be live entertainment, a fireworks show, Santa Claus, and apparently enough twinkling lights to illuminate three Rodeo Drive blocks.

It was an excellent opportunity to network with all the City of Beverly Hills officials and demonstrate how enthusiastic they were to be part of the community. She'd already chatted with Dave about an after-party at Belcanto after next year's event.

A text notification popped up from Dave. Her smile disappeared. *There's an accident on the 405 and I'm stuck in traffic. No way can I make it, so you and Lucas make sure to circulate and schmooze. Sorry.*

Zut, alors. She and Lucas hadn't been alone together since the day she'd told him she wanted to "keep it simple." And now they were going to spend the evening alone together at a festive holiday event? Tonight would test if they could act like friendly colleagues.

It would be fine. After all, they'd only spent one night together, and weeks had passed.

She headed toward Lucas's office, but when she peeked in, it was empty. Had he left without her? She strolled to the lobby and paused to admire the breathtaking, elegant space.

Black and white Italian marble tile floors imparted European flair, robin's egg blue velvet couches encircling the marble columns complemented the Post-Impressionistic art adorning the alabaster walls beautifully. The late afternoon light streamed through the floor-to-ceiling glass entrance doors, gleaming off the polished reception desk. In other words, perfection.

"Brigitte."

She turned and drank in his handsome, square-jawed face. Her breath hitched and a wave of longing whispered though her. "There you are. I was looking for you, did you get a text from Dave, too?"

"I did, so it looks like you and I are representing Paramount tonight. Are you ready?" Neither his tone nor his neutral expression gave anything away.

So they were acting like polite co-workers. She offered a small smile. "I am. Let's go."

Together they exited the hotel and when Brigitte

stepped onto the polished sidewalk, a group of revelers bumped into her, and she stumbled. Lucas caught her around the waist before she went down. Despite the layers of her cashmere sweater and leather jacket, his large hands seared her as if his long fingers were touching her bare skin.

He drew her back against his muscular frame. When his clean masculine scent filled her nostrils, a lick of heat curled down her spine.

She inhaled a shaky breath and angled her gaze up at him. "You've saved me from falling again. Thank you."

He hadn't released her, and the protective circle of his arms felt too good, too strong, too secure for her to move. Not yet.

Concern etched along his forehead and his bottle green eyes narrowed. "Will you be okay with all the people?"

"The people?" His beautiful mouth was inches from hers and if she stood on her tiptoes, she could kiss him. Could wind her arms around his neck and press herself against him. Awareness simmered between them.

His pupils flared and his hands tightened before he released her and stepped back. "Well, I wasn't sure if being stuck in a crowd would make you feel claustrophobic."

She inhaled a fortifying breath. "You're so thoughtful. Thank you. But we're out in the fresh air so even though it's busy, I don't feel trapped."

He studied her for another moment. "Okay, if you're sure. It's packed out here tonight so stay close and let me lead the way over to the stage area. That's where several of the City council folks will be."

Together they navigated the noisy, bustling crowd. Well, to be accurate, Lucas's broad shoulders forged a path through the throngs. Glimmering lights added a magical feel to downtown Beverly Hills, like they were in a Swiss ski village. Her new town really did have that European feel that gave her a feeling of familiarity.

She stayed close and worked to regulate her racing heart. Being in close proximity with Lucas for the first time since they'd slept together had her nervous system on high alert. She resisted the temptation to intertwine her fingers with his.

Every night for the last few weeks, she'd replay their hot night together. The feel of his skin like silk over steel, the passion of his kisses, the way he filled her like he was made just for her. It would be so easy to hold onto him, to rely on his strength, but they'd made their boundaries crystal clear.

Regret tugged at her because right now? The reasons he'd enumerated why it was smarter for them to keep their relationship professional evaded her. They were adults, they could be discreet. At least she could and right now, she couldn't think of one reason why they shouldn't try.

Didn't she pride herself on living life in the present moment? Time to do something about this situation––they'd both benefit. Mind made up, she caught Lucas's arm, pulled him to a stop in front of the stage's outer perimeter where long, festively decorated tables were set up with refreshments. Fat potted poinsettias and mugs brimming with hot cocoa and apple cider adorned the one closest to them.

She gazed up and pressed one hand against his solid chest. "Can I buy you a drink?"

He inhaled sharply. "Buy me a drink?"

"Hot chocolate to warm you up? It's chilly out here tonight." She picked up two mugs and offered one to him.

"I'm pretty sure it's complimentary but cocoa sounds good." He reached for the drink and his hand brushed hers, sending a shiver through her.

They sipped their steaming chocolate and the festivities fell away. Something about being with Lucas made her feel like they were in their own little bubble. And she liked it. She'd never felt connected to a man this way.

The bubble burst when a middle-aged Black man slapped Lucas on the back. "Lucas Sutton, so glad to see you here. I'm Will Chance, the City Manager, we've spoken on the phone. We're excited to have Paramount open soon. It'll be great for the city."

And that's how it went for the next hour. More members of the City Council, the local Sheriff, a few of the boutique owners, and more people than Brigitte could place chatted with them. Lucas was confident and friendly with everyone. Between the two of them, they made a damn good impression, if she did say so herself.

After the impressive fireworks display, the happy crowd dispersed.

"Well, you two are the perfect pair to represent Paramount. I'm impressed. Now, I'm heading off for a late dinner and you should do the same. Looking forward to the hotel's soft launch next month. Thanks so much for the invitation." The Mayor shook both their hands before strolling away.

"I guess that's our cue. Can I give you a ride home?" Lucas's auburn hair was tousled, his lean cheeks flushed from the breeze, and he looked heart-breakingly handsome.

Carpe diem. "Yes, but only if you come home with me." She held her breath.

His jaw tightened. "Brigitte, we——"

She pressed one finger against his lips, savored the way he went still. "We're good together, the Mayor even said so. I can't stop thinking about you. And if I don't have you inside me soon, I may lose my mind."

His eyes hooded, he clasped her jaw in one hand, and slanted his mouth across hers. She moaned and wound her arms around his neck. He tasted like chocolate, and mint, and desire. Heat bloomed low in her belly.

"Damn it, I can't resist you. Let's go." He caught her hand in his powerful grip and pivoted toward their hotel.

She had to canter to keep up with him. If she tripped, she knew he wouldn't let her fall. He'd proven that repeatedly. They reached his sleek gunmetal gray Mercedes and when he opened her door, she plastered herself against his powerful back, and slid her arms around him.

He growled. "If you keep touching me like that, we'll end up in the back seat."

"You do have a nice back seat…but take me home. And hurry." Too bad the hotel wasn't open yet, or she would drag him to one of the rooms.

They dove into the car, and he rocketed through the unusually quiet streets. She stroked his leg, but he caught her hand, holding hers still. "My glasses are already fogging up and I'll wrap us around a tree if you don't stop. We're almost there."

"Faster," she purred, savoring the heat combusting between them.

He peeled into a parking space in front of her building, and they leapt out of the car. He scooped her up in his arms, captured her mouth with his, and jogged up the stairs to her second-floor condo. She fumbled in her purse for the keys and leaned down to unlock the door. He shoved it open, slammed it behind them, and carried her to the kitchen island and set her on the smooth granite.

"I need to take you hard. Is that okay?" He murmured against the sensitive skin of her neck before raking his teeth along her collarbone and lightly biting down.

She shivered and drove her fingers into his thick hair. "Yes, right here. Now."

He released her and helped her out of her pants, shoving them off and kicking them to the side. He grabbed a condom from his wallet, shoved his slacks to his knees, and entered her in one thrust.

She wrapped her legs around his waist and held on for the ride. He took her in long, masterful strokes, his hands gripping her hips, keeping her in place. Their breath came in ferocious pants, his forehead pressed to hers. She was surrounded by him, filled by him, and the waves of pleasure flowed through her building to a burst of fireworks brighter than the ones earlier tonight. He captured her mouth and kissed her as they both came apart.

"Umm, wow."

He laughed, his voice husky. "Wow is one word for it. I guess we needed that."

He eased back, kicked off his shoes, and stepped out of his pants, which were around his ankles.

"Let's go to my room for round two. But let me take off my coat and scarf first." She looked down at herself and giggled––naked from the waist down, cashmere scarf intact.

His pupils flared. "Woman, you'll kill me, but I can't think of a better way to go." He picked her up again, carried her to her bedroom, and she tossed her clothes aside. He eased them down onto her king-sized bed.

She turned onto her side and rested her cheek in her hands, admiring the sheen of sweat highlighting all his sinewy muscles as he stretched out beside her. Funny, she'd never really cared much about muscles until Lucas. Now she could absolutely count herself as a convert. At least with him.

His green eyes were hooded, his hair sticking up all around his handsome face, and he looked relaxed. *"Tu as l'air très content de soi."*

"Does that mean I've died and gone to heaven?" He brushed his thumb across her lower lip, then cradled her face in one strong hand.

She turned and pressed a kiss against his palm. "More like the cat who swallowed the cream, but *oui*, you look happy."

"You make me happy." His gaze was penetrating.

Her heart skipped a beat and she worked to keep her tone light. "Meaning you've got that post-sex glow happy?"

A small crease appeared between his brows. "It's not the sex. Well, not just the sex. I feel good when I'm around you. You're the most interesting woman I've ever met. You're passionate and intelligent, and so confident--you're a force. I've missed you these last weeks."

Her heart lurched in her chest, and she shivered. "I've missed you, too. I…" Damn it, she would be brave. "I feel safe with you, protected."

"Safe? That sounds boring." He frowned.

She inhaled a fortifying breath, reached for his hand, and intertwined her fingers with his. "*Non*, not safe in a boring way. Safe in that I feel I can share more of myself with you. Be vulnerable. I'm so used to being independent and on my own, I'm not used to letting anyone close to me. But with you, I feel I can let my guard down and you won't judge me. You don't expect me to always be 'on.'"

"You don't need to be perfect around me because I sure as hell am far from it." He squeezed her hand.

"Can we simply be together and see what happens?"

"Yeah. I was probably more distracted not seeing you than I would be if we were seeing each other." He hesitated for a moment, then blew out a breath. "I'm falling for you, Brigitte. Does that make you want to run?"

Joy bloomed inside her. "*Non*, I want to stay. Here in Beverly Hills. Here with you. I've never felt this way before about anyone. I'm crazy about you."

His face lit up and he pulled her into his arms. His kiss was tender, gentle, and warm.

"I'm going to make love to you now, and I'm going to take

my time. I'm going to show you what a goddess you are." He brushed his parted lips down her neck, and goosebumps to erupt along her skin.

"Lucas," she whispered and arched her back to get closer.

"Let me worship you." He traveled lower, torturing her with his thoroughness, his talented tongue and masterful hands.

No man had touched her so reverently, with so much tenderness and attention. They made slow, exquisite love and after they came apart together, she lay cradled in his powerful arms, her heart cracking wide open.

Could this feeling really last?

CHAPTER 19

$\mathcal{D}$ecember 1st

"Are you sure we don't have time to run back to your place? Or sneak back into my office without anyone seeing us?" Brigitte leaned in across the table, a wicked glint in her gray-blue eyes.

Lucas's mind whirred through the possibilities. Maybe? "You know there's a million people swarming around the hotel now, and Jon arrives this afternoon."

She sat back and pouted. "Where's your sense of adventure?"

"Oh, I'll show you adventure tonight." He waggled his eyebrows.

She giggled. "You're very naughty. Just like every night. And you're right. Besides, your favorite interior designer is here all week. Dagmar asked about you."

He rolled his eyes. "Yeah, right. I've already got Jon scheduled with her. He'll have her wrapped around his finger and I will hopefully never have to see her again."

The waiter reappeared with their coffees and the bill. Once he disappeared, Lucas leaned back in the café chair and crossed an ankle over his knee. The last few weeks had been a whirlwind of long hours at Paramount and longer nights with Brigitte. They'd settled into a rhythm of work and pleasure, and he'd never been happier.

She clanked her coffee cup against his. "I'll toast to that. Anything else I can do for you today?"

"Just keep doing what you're doing. You're doing an excellent job." Between Brigitte and Dave, he'd been able to focus on budgets and forecasting numbers, which was his sweet spot.

She tapped one slender finger against her red lips. "Hmm, does that mean I'm up for a bonus, boss?"

How he'd been more productive over these last few weeks than he'd ever been before was beyond him. "Oh, maybe we can negotiate a bonus."

"Oh really? Hmmm, well in the meantime, if we aren't having a quickie on my desk, perhaps I'll settle for a kiss?"

The visual of her bent over the desk, her skirt shoved up around her waist, her long legs spread wide washed over him, and he was rock hard. Again. He adjusted his slacks.

"Your desk is a paper mountain––that would never work. And we both have back to back meetings the rest of the day. But why don't we meet at my place at the dining room table?" He made a show of glancing at his Tag Heuer. "At 9:00 tonight?"

Her pupils flared. "9:00 works for me. And my desk isn't that bad."

He chuckled. "Sure. And it's a date. But we should get back. I don't want to be late meeting Jon."

They finished their coffees and strolled back to Paramount hand in hand. Brigitte expounded on an idea she'd had for the soft launch packages for the following weekend. She waved her free hand around, the way she always spoke when she was excited about something.

The sun reflected off her shiny mahogany hair and contentment filled him. He had more energy, more confidence, and sure as hell more satisfaction with her by his side. Somehow working with her helped him cope with the parts of the job he still disliked. And the romantic nights? He was all in.

The more time they spent together, the deeper he fell. Like Brigitte said, life was short and meant to be lived in the present moment.

He pulled her into his arms. "I didn't want to forget to give you that kiss."

She curled her fingers into the crisp fabric of his shirt and lifted her face. "Kiss me."

He framed her exquisite face in his hands and slanted his mouth across hers. Her impossibly soft lips parted on a sigh and their tongues teased and tangled in a lazy dance. She tasted sweet like café au lait, mingled with her own unique flavor.

Reluctantly, he lifted his head and exhaled an unsteady breath. This woman had him spinning. "Satisfied?"

Her lips curved into a feline smile. "For now."

He stared down at her for a moment, words escaping him. Yeah, he was falling head over heels in love with Brigitte Thibault. Maybe they hadn't said the words yet, but he knew she was falling for him, too. They spent every day and every night together and each day was sweeter than the last. It was only a matter of time.

"Lucas?" She tilted her head. "You okay?"

He smiled. "I'm just happy. You make me happy."

Her dark fan of lashes lowered, and her lips curved upwards. "Me, too. Very happy."

His heart warmed and he linked his fingers with hers. "And on that note, we should get back to the hotel."

"Well, well, well, if it isn't Lucas and Brigitte looking mighty cozy." A coy voice said from behind them.

They whirled around and there stood Jon, right next to them. "Jon, we didn't expect to see you yet."

Jon smoothed down his impeccably tailored royal blue suit, and grinned. "Obviously. I mean, if you don't want me, believe me, I could do some damage on Rodeo Drive this afternoon. The shopping here is fabulous."

Brigitte stepped up and kissed Jon's cheeks. "Oh darling, you and I will get along famously. Charlie did say the main reason you wanted the job up here was because of the shopping."

Lucas laughed. "Neither of you are going shopping now. And Jon, I need you. Now I can sit back, put my feet up, and have a beer."

"Oh honey, I don't think so. But seriously, let's get started. I'm ready to slay."

"Shall we head inside?" Brigitte asked.

Huh, funny, Lucas hadn't notice they were a few doors down from Paramount. And was it bad he didn't really care that they'd kissed near the hotel's entrance?

Jon's gaze sharpened and his smile turned sly. "Before we go inside––spill the deets. How long has this been going on?"

Brigitte stiffened. "Now Jon, what ever could you mean?"

"Oh please. Tell me all the details. You two are in love, aren't you? Just like we all predicted." Jon pointed at them, a shit-eating grin on his face. "I think it's fantastic. Keeping it all in the family. Now, Ryan and Charlie haven't breathed a word to me about it. Have you two been keeping this a secret? I knew not to bet against you."

Lucas shrugged and ignored the flush creeping up his neck. "Not on purpose. It's been so hectic and there really hasn't been time to discuss anything but the launch. But we're not keeping it secret, if that's what you mean. Screw the bet, we don't care about that, do we?"

"*Non*, we don't care about the bet. But please don't say anything. I want to tell Charlie myself. And we figured the soft launch might be a good time to let everyone know." Brigitte stepped away from him.

Jon clapped his hands together. "Well, you better do it then because no way am I sitting on this juicy news. And now we just need to find me the man of my dreams."

"I'm sure you'll have no problem meeting him. But first, why don't we get to work. Let's go get you settled in your office," Lucas said.

Jon sniffed. "It better be bigger than that shoebox Ryan stuffed me in down at Pacific Jewel Inn."

"On that note, I'll leave you two. I've got an appointment in ten minutes." Brigitte gave a half wave and strolled away.

Lucas and Jon stood and watched the gentle sway of her hips as she left. Damn, she was gorgeous.

"I'm proud of you. That's one incredible woman. Has she been doing as good a job as Charlie claims?"

"She's incredible. I don't know what I'd have done without her, especially before Dave got here. She's so smooth and confident, and man, does she get stuff done. You should see some of these arrangements she negotiated, like with Private Suite at LAX and--"

"Lucas Sutton, you are smitten. I love it. And I know she's been doing a lot of my duties so I'm grateful. Now show me my office."

Lucas flushed but found he didn't care who recognized he was gone over Brigitte. "Like I said, she's amazing. Let's go."

They entered the hotel and Jon oohed and aahed through

the elegant lobby, past the reception desk, and down the hallway to Jon's new office. "It's the same size as my office, you've got a huge window, the office furniture you chose is already set up, and I assume you've got your laptop."

Jon gave a whoop. "Yes, this is fantastic. Finally, an office that suits me. Thanks, I love it. What do you need me to start with? Belcanto? Front desk? Any of the renovations not completed properly yet?"

Lucas sighed. "I'm so glad you're here. You know I prefer the back office work, so I'm relieved to have you here as my right-hand person. I'll have you deal with Dagmar on some of the finishing touches on the interior design. She's been a royal pain in the ass so thank god Brigitte's been handling her up until now."

Jon threw himself into the cherry-red desk chair and swiveled around. "You know I thrive on challenges. What else?"

"Go ahead and look at the schedule for this week. You've got a long to-do list and I'll send Dave down if he's free. And will you be up for dinner at 6:30 with Dave, Brigitte, and me? We're refining plans for next weekend's soft opening."

"Dinner sounds perfect, and I already picked out my suite for the launch evening. From what I've seen, it looks like you've got everything on track, and I think the soft launch idea is brilliant."

Lucas leaned against the misty gray colored wall and crossed his arms. "I wasn't sure at first, but I think the soft launch will really help us make any last minute tweaks. I know we didn't do it for any of the other hotels, but Beverly Hills clientele are a special breed."

"Like I said, I like it. Paramount is going to be the best hotel yet. It has to be because I've given Ryan reams of crap telling him so. Especially now I've been promoted and you're running the show." Jon grinned.

"See you later. Call me if you need anything." Lucas closed Jon's door behind him and pushed his glasses back up the bridge of his nose on the way back to his office.

With Jon's impressive organizational skills, his ability to handle any annoying personality thrown at him, and his sheer knowledge of the day to day operations, he would be a better G.M. than him. He had a natural gift for the hospitality industry. Like Brigitte.

Yeah, somehow everything circled back to her. He laughed to himself and massaged the back of his neck. If this was what falling in love felt like, he understood why his friends were so happy. He and Brigitte hadn't said the words yet, but actions spoke louder than words, right?

And why was the idea of having Jon take over so tempting?

Although he was doing a good job so far, he had to admit he missed working primarily with facts and figures. Sure, he could run the hotel and he hadn't royally screwed anything up so far, but it wasn't a natural fit for him like it was with the others. Ryan and Jack were naturals.

Cam's transition from an Army Captain had been smooth because his leadership skills were ingrained. Hell, even Austin had been the lead singer of Black Velvet Machine and run a bar, so he was accustomed to dealing with the public.

Was he doing this because he was passionate about it or was it more to keep up his end of the bargain with his best friends? Brigitte talked a lot about living life in the present moment and the importance of being passionate about what you were doing. So was he? With that nugget ping-ponging around his brain, he returned to his office and shut the door.

For now, he was launching this damn hotel, and this was just stress. Of course he wanted to run Paramount. The last few weeks had been so busy, of course he was feeling pressured. And he didn't even feel bad that he'd fallen in line with the rest of them and fallen in love with his employee. He hadn't confided in any of the guys yet because well, it wasn't like they sat around and discussed their feelings.

No, for now he'd focus on ensuring the soft launch was a huge success.

CHAPTER 20

*B*rigitte closed her office door, crossed to the window, and stared at the picture perfect view. An unfamiliar wave of nerves flooded her system. Although her afternoon meetings had gone smoothly, she'd been distracted.

She pressed her hands against her churning belly. Now that Jon knew about her and Lucas, it was time to stop procrastinating and tell Charlie. She'd never kept secrets from her best friend before. Even if she and Lucas were taking it day by day, even if it was temporary, Charlie deserved to know. She squared her shoulders and fished her phone out of her purse.

Before she could make the call her phone rang. Business first.

"*Bonjour, puis-je parler avec* Brigitte Thibault?"

"*Bonjour, c'est* Brigitte."

"Hello, it's Tracee Leduq checking in with you again. How's everything going there in Beverly Hills?"

Ah, the recruiter again. The woman was nothing if not persistent. "Everything is excellent, thank you. We've got our soft launch coming up this weekend and the grand opening on New Year's Eve."

"Hmm, and are you still keeping the offer in mind for next year? Once you've completed your duties launching Paramount?"

Brigitte cleared her throat. "I'm very happy here." With work. With Lucas. With life. For now, anyway.

"I'm sure it's lovely but it can't compare to this opportunity. You would have the chance for something truly one of a kind, something where you would make your mark in the industry."

Brigitte couldn't help but be flattered. She'd worked hard to be the best and to be pursued individually for this type of dream job felt like validation. If they had contacted her before she'd accepted the Paramount job, she likely would have jumped at the chance, Charlie or no Charlie.

Because the assignments were short, it guaranteed she wouldn't need to worry about getting bored and wanting to move somewhere new. Like she had every single time. *Just like her mother.*

But for the first time, because of the Hotel Kings unconditional acceptance, she was part of a family. Paramount was different. *She* was different. And her feelings for Lucas were different.

Her gut tightened. He hadn't said, "I love you." Sure, they'd said they were crazy about each other but who knew what would happen when the initial honeymoon phase ended? There were no guarantees it would last.

She exhaled an unsteady breath. "Tracee, I appreciate the offer. I'm going to stay."

"Brigitte, look, they really want you. And don't forget, this offer is more than double what you're making now. If it's money, I'm sure they will allow you to write your ticket if you come on board. You don't have any ties to Beverly Hills, do you?"

"Again, I appreciate it and I'm sure there are several candidates just as or more qualified than me. The answer is no." But did she really have ties? It had only been a few months. Was she making a mistake?

Tracee huffed. "Okay. They anticipated you not deciding until after Paramount opens. All you need to do is call me, they will send the company jet for you, you can see the first property, meet the owner, and decide from there. May I call you again just in case you change your mind?"

She nibbled on her lower lip. She should say no but, what came out was, "Okay, fine."

"*A bientôt.*"

"*Au revoir*, Tracee." Brigitte tossed her phone onto her desk and sank into the blue velvet armchair across from it.

This dream job offer was like some kind of bizarre universal test or something. The perfect role for a nomad who bored easily and was always seeking...something more. In the past, she would have been in the buttery leather seat of their private jet straight away.

But when Charlie took the job in La Jolla and then fell in love with Ryan and started a new life, a life not merely based on professional accomplishments, travel, and the pursuit of pleasure, her perspective began to change.

Except for each other, she and Charlie hadn't been in relationships where another person truly had their back. Loved them and protected them and believed in them. Seeing her best friend's transformation from merely happy to happy and fulfilled and supported had been confusing at first.

But now with Lucas, she was experiencing a taste of how it felt. And she was addicted.

And it scared the hell out of her.

Because she was relaxing into their relationship, she thought about Lucas all the time, she wanted him all the time. And she was falling in love with him. She'd never said, "I love you," to a man before. Never felt it. Never meant it.

Lucas made her believe she could have it all. And the terrifying thing was now she did want it all. With him. To stay in Beverly Hills. To try. Her heart hammered in her chest.

She grabbed her phone. Time to call Charlie and tell her that she and Lucas were together. Ask her how she navigated the terror that surged through her veins at being truly vulnerable.

Charlie's phone went straight to voicemail. Immediately, a text popped up.

> Sorry, can't talk right now. Everything is bananas until we come up for the launch on Saturday night. Can we catch up then?

Brigitte closed her eyes. *Merde.*

She could say it was urgent, just to get it off her chest but Charlie was slammed with end-of-the year and working with Dave on the Paramount marketing plans. *Non,* she could handle it herself. Plenty of time to talk to Charlie before Saturday.

> Okay. Can't wait to see you. But if you have a moment before then, text me.

> Of course! 🩶

Her phone buzzed again. *Lucas.*

> Counting down the hours until dinner and can't wait to have you for dessert.

Joy sparked through her. This strong, sweet, adorable

man sent the cutest messages. She stuffed the job offer deep into the vault--everything would work out fine.

~

"Okay, Dave and Jon are great, but they can sure talk." Lucas lay on his side, his head propped in one large hand.

She laughed and brushed her fingers along his square jaw. "And talk. I know. I was afraid they'd kick us out of Crustacean."

He grinned and stroked his hand along her bare skin and goosebumps rose. "The waitress must have come by five times hinting for us to leave. Anyway, here we are."

"Here we are. Did you get enough dessert?" They had sped back to her place once they'd finally been able to get out of the restaurant without making a scene.

Now they were both sweaty, satiated, and snuggled together on her smooth sheets.

His lips twitched. "For now. But you know I've developed quite a sweet tooth lately." His long fingers curled around her hip.

"Mmm, me, too. And are we all set for this weekend? We've got the 'romance package' booked and that's how we're telling everyone? Right?"

He exhaled. "Yeah, let's just rip off the Band-aid. There will be reams of crap and money flying around for the bet, but I don't care."

Her heart squeezed in her chest. "I feel the same. And you're feeling good about Paramount? I think we're going to blow everyone away with this launch. The guys won't be able to dispute Paramount is the best hotel yet. And that's on you."

His emerald eyes widened. "On me?"

She pressed her palm against his heart, loving the steady rhythm beneath her hand. "Yes, on you. You're fantastic as

General Manager and I can't wait for everyone to acknowledge it."

"I couldn't have done it without you, and the guys, and Dave. But I'm just not sure..." his gaze flicked away, somewhere over her shoulder.

"Not sure?"

"I need to tell you something and I'm not sure you're going to like it."

Her throat tightened. He'd just told her he was happy with her. With them. What could it be?

"And can you promise it stays between us? Not even a word to Charlie?"

"Of course." She swallowed, her throat suddenly parched. More secrets?

He turned, sat up, and raked his hands through his thick hair. "Look, I think I've done a good job. I know the launch will be successful. Paramount will be successful. I *can* do this job, which I wasn't sure of even a few months ago. But the thing is, I'm not sure I *want* to keep doing it."

"What?"

He looked at her now, his brow furrowed, his jaw tight. "Look, when we were young and came up with this idea, it seemed like a dream come true. And then Ryan became a force in the industry, and we all pooled our various talents, and hell, we never could have imagined it would be so successful.

"But the thing is, I love being the finance guy. I don't like a lot of the duties as head of the hotel. You've got all the skills. Jon's got all the skills. All I'm saying is just because I can do it, I don't know that this is what I want to do long-term."

She scooted closer and linked her fingers with his. "Lucas, are you sure this isn't pre-opening pressure? Do you think this feeling will calm down once the hotel is open?"

"I don't think so. One thing you've taught me in a short time is to live in the present moment more. That I can combine work and pleasure, and everything won't come crashing down. And I just think I'd rather be CFO instead of the face of Paramount. But I don't know how to break that to Ryan and the guys. To let them all down. After everything." He groaned and dropped his head in his hands.

She pressed up onto her knees and massaged the tight cords of muscle in his neck. "Do you really think you doing another role is letting them down? I mean, I believe in you and you're doing a great job, but I also believe in doing what makes you happiest. That's why I prefer to be the concierge, even when Ryan was pushing me to take the Assistant G.M. role. Are you going to say something this weekend?"

"That feels incredible. I'll tell him after the opening. I committed to doing it and I will. Although I just feel like I'm messing up his grand plans."

"Yes, well you have grand plans, too. And Ryan and the guys are your best friends, your brothers as you call them. They want you to be happy, first and foremost."

He sighed and sat up, turned his head to her. "You're amazing, you know that? And maybe you're right. Maybe once we're through the launch, it will all be fine."

"I have just the thing to help you feel better." She licked her lips.

His eyes hooded immediately. "Oh yeah?"

"Just lie back and I'll show you." She pressed against his chest, and he sank back against the mound of pillows.

A rush of pure power flooded through her as she looked down at him. This gorgeous, sensitive man was hers and she was going to please herself by pleasuring him.

His chest rumbled. "Brigitte."

She stroked her hands down his chiseled, hard torso, then leaned down and pressed an open-mouth kiss on his chest and continued nibbling and tasting. Savoring his clean masculine scent mingled with the sweat from their earlier lovemaking.

She curled one hand around him and slid her mouth over him, taking her time as she kissed, and caressed, and licked. His hips jerked and he cried out her name, his fingers thrusting into her hair. She smiled against his velvety skin. Yes, he wouldn't worry any more tonight.

Everything else could wait.

CHAPTER 21

*D*ecember 10*th*, *Paramount Soft Launch*

"TONIGHT HAS BEEN PERFECT——YOU knocked this out of the park, Lucas." Ryan smacked him on the back. "And this is only a preview of how epic the New Year's Eve grand opening will be. Thanks."

His spirits soared, buoyed by his best friend and boss's praise. Ryan wasn't exactly effusive or generous with compliments, so it meant a lot to hear the words. It boosted his confidence for Paramount's potential success.

He surveyed the high-ceilinged lobby, which after two hours of cocktail hour was still buzzing with lively chatter, twinkling lights, and gorgeous people dressed in their finest evening wear. "Thanks. I don't know if everything is perfect but it's pretty damn good. And thanks for letting me do the soft launch."

"I know you're cautious and now that I see how well this is going, in retrospect we should have done it for the other hotels. The crowd is happy, Santiago killed it with catering just enough food to keep everyone full, and the red carpet and a photographer at the entrance is a great idea. We're doing that for the grand opening, too, right?" Ryan asked.

He nodded and waved at the Mayor, who lounged on one of the Tiffany-box-blue velvet couches, chatting with Jack. "That was Brigitte's idea and yeah, we will. When in L.A., we cater to the crowd."

"What was my idea?" A hint of warm floral fragrance reached him a second before Brigitte materialized at his side and pressed one small hand against his shoulder. He turned to look at her and his heart tightened. She was so fucking breathtaking. How had he gotten so lucky?

Tonight, her dark hair was sleek and straight, to go with the single-column silver sheath dress slit up to her toned-mid thigh. Her scarlet lips were curved into a satisfied smile, and she gestured with her champagne flute.

Ryan smiled at her. "The red carpet. Love making it feel like a Hollywood première. Everyone's having a great time and no glitches so far, right?"

"So far, so good. And while I am excellent at my job, Lucas deserves the credit for pulling this all together, three weeks before the opening. We've got all the rooms full with local influencers and a few city council members. And of course some of the rooms are ours." Brigitte leaned against him.

A quick flare of heat shot through him, and he caught her hand, linking their fingers together. "I couldn't have done this without you."

Charlie joined them and threaded one arm through Ryan's. "There you are. Tonight is amazing. You should hear the buzz out there––people love the old-school elegant vibe in here. Paramount is going to be one of the best in Beverly Hills, for sure."

Ryan smiled and gave Charlie a quick kiss. "I did tell him that and I'm feeling pretty damn proud of all of us for pulling off this whole endeavor. And then I was about to ask if it's too soon to say, "I told you so"?"

Brigitte gave her throaty laugh. "You mean, I told you so, Lucas you'd be great as G.M. of Paramount?"

Ryan rolled his eyes. "That was never a question in my mind."

"I appreciate the confidence because I wasn't so sure myself," Lucas said.

Charlie grinned. "No goofball, we all knew you and Brigitte would get together. Nobody bet against it. After every other hotel opening turned into a love story, there was no way you two could resist."

"Yeah, you didn't have a chance." Ryan laughed.

"Well, once I saw Lucas on the rugby field, I didn't stand a chance...all those muscles." Brigitte made a show of squeezing his biceps. "Ooh, la la."

And now his ears were on fire. He gazed down into her eyes. "You mean I didn't stand a chance."

"Okay, you two are adorable. And way to make the announcement by booking the Romance Package. And now I know my best friend will be living in the same state as me forever. My evil plan worked." Charlie rubbed her hands together.

"Stop teasing them, Charlie." Ryan shook his head. "Come on, let's go catch up with Cam and Lucy. But yeah, you two lost the hell out of the bet."

"I can't help myself. And I need to run to the powder room first. Brigitte, come with me." Charlie grabbed Brigitte's arm and led her away.

"Okay, you're serious about her, aren't you?" Ryan asked.

Lucas nodded. "Yeah. Yeah, I am. I can't freakin' believe she's into me but I'm in love with her."

"That's great. I'm happy for you guys and I know Charlie's thrilled. Look at us, all running our hotels and in long-term relationships. Everything we talked about all those years ago came true."

Lucas paused and looked around. Shit. While he didn't want to burst the bubble, an overwhelming urge to tell Ryan how he felt coursed through him. Ryan was his brother from another mother, and they'd always been honest with each other. And he didn't want to wait.

He inhaled a steadying breath. "Hey, can we talk for a minute in the Cigar and Whiskey Lounge? I need to tell you something."

A crease appeared between Ryan's eyebrows. "Everything okay?"

"Yeah. But let's talk in private. I'm meeting with the City Manager in a while and want to run something by you first." Now or never.

They entered the empty lounge. "Do you want a whiskey? I've got the key to the liquor cabinet."

Ryan laughed. "Like when we opened your parents' liquor cabinet that summer after sophomore year?"

"Um, no. My parents had that crappy stuff--not exactly top shelf whiskies. But have a seat."

"Now you're freaking me out. What is it?" Ryan sat on the edge of one of the couches, his jaw tight.

Lucas sat across from him. "Okay, just let me get this all out before you say anything. I know your dream is to run our hotel chain and for each of us to run our own hotel. We're more successful than any of us could have predicted. But I..."

"But?"

"But now that we're in it," he took a deep breath. "I know this isn't my dream and I--"

Ryan surged to his feet; his eyes wide. "What?"

Lucas held up a hand. "Let me finish. I think I've done a

good job for pre-launch but the thing is, while I can do this, it's not natural for me. There are so many parts of being G.M. that stress me the fuck out."

"Yeah, but some of that's just because it's new. It will come over time. And Jon's here now. Dude, you've done an amazing job."

"Thanks. I have done a good job but it's less about me being able to do it and more about me wanting to do it. I miss working with the numbers. Working on forecasting and projections. The rest of it is just…" He massaged the back of his neck.

Ryan sank back onto the leather sofa. "You're serious."

"Yeah, I know we've talked about this for years. I know everyone else is happy in their roles and I don't want to fuck this up for everyone but I'm just not all in and we need someone who is to run Paramount. I'm sorry." His gut tightened––damn it, he didn't want to let his friends down, but he needed to be true to himself.

Ryan rose and strode over to the glass-walled display case, studied the whiskies and cigars. "So what do you want to do?"

He couldn't take back the words now. Might as well share what he'd been contemplating. "Well, of course I'll make sure launch goes through and stay as acting G.M. until we have a replacement. But now all the hotels are open, I'd like to transition into the CFO role."

Ryan's back was still to him, but the tension in his shoulders softened. "So you want to stay, just not run Paramount."

"Of course I want to stay. I just don't want my own hotel." Or deal with all the Dagmars and Filipoviches.

Ryan whirled around and pointed a finger at him. "I have an idea. How about Brigitte as G.M.? She'd be great."

He stiffened. "Brigitte's happy as concierge."

"She's wasted in that role. The woman is a leader and why

wouldn't she want to run it? You guys are together now, Charlie's close by. It's perfect."

"Dude, this is my point. Just because someone is good at something doesn't mean it fulfills them. I can do the role and don't want to do it. Brigitte's made her boundaries really clear by turning down the Assistant G.M. job more than once. Why would you assume she'd want even more responsibility than that?"

Ryan shrugged. "Charlie told me Brigitte's never really settled anywhere and likes to leave her options open. It seems like she's settled here in California. Settled here being with you."

"Look, I'm in love with her and I want her to be happy. If it's something she wants, of course. What about Jon?"

"Well, he just got promoted to Assistant G.M. and I know he wants to run his own hotel one day. He's made that clear."

"And he's worked with you for the last two years--learned from you and Charlie. He's only been here a couple of weeks and he's a natural. Hell, he understands the job better than me."

Ryan's lips twitched. "Dude, he probably knows it better than any of us. What if you stepped down to Assistant G.M.? Just switch roles?"

"No. Use me where I can help Hotel Kings the most."

"Okay, how about this. You said you understand Brigitte best. Why don't you see where her head is now that you two are together. If you guys end up like me and Charlie, she's here forever. And from the get-go, we've wanted her as Assistant G.M. or even G.M. if that's what she wanted. Maybe her perspective on it has changed. It's worth asking, right?"

"You've got a point. I'll open the discussion but I'm not pushing her. But I'll make sure we've got my replacement in place before I step away, deal?"

Because no way would he pressure Brigitte. She was used to being on her own. She wasn't used to someone having her back. Part of why he hadn't told her he loved her yet was he didn't want to scare her away. Didn't want to ask her for too much, too soon. He was a patient man.

"Got it. And Lucas, of course I'm disappointed that the master plan we made fifteen years ago isn't ending up exactly as we planned, but I love you like a brother and I want you to be happy. We'll figure it out." Ryan stood and pulled him for a one-armed hug.

Emotion welled in his chest and he exhaled a relieved sigh. "Thanks. I love you, too, brother."

Ryan stepped back. "Okay, I'm going to go find my wife. You coming?"

"Nah, the City Manager is meeting me here," he paused and glanced down at his watch. "In five minutes. I'm just going to enjoy the quiet for a minute."

"Great. I'll see you later." Ryan turned and strolled back to the festivities.

Lucas sank into the couch and dropped his head back onto the cushion. He'd done it--come clean with Ryan. It was all going to work out and he hadn't ruined their hotel chain and hadn't ruined their friendship. Best of all, he'd be free to do what he loved best.

He couldn't wait to tell Brigitte the good news. If not for her encouragement, he might have continued to suffer in silence. Brigitte had changed his life in more ways than one and he couldn't wait to spend the rest of his life with her.

CHAPTER 22

"I have to say, if someone had told me before you moved here that you'd end up with Lucas, I would have laughed. But you look really happy." Charlie smiled at their reflections in mirror.

Brigitte touched up her lipstick before responding. "I am happy, truly happy. He's amazing. But while we have a minute, I need to tell you about a job offer I received."

"A job offer? You promised you would stay. I know we haven't seen each other as much as we'd hoped but we can do better once the hotel launches. And what about Lucas? I thought you guys were in love?"

Brigitte flicked her hand in the air. "See, that's the thing. You just automatically assumed I'd take it. Everyone assumes I can't stick anywhere."

Charlie frowned. "Hey, that's not fair. You've said you never found your forever place. You didn't want the Assistant G.M. role, even when we asked you again when I was here last time. You made it pretty clear the jury was still out on California feeling like home."

"You're my best friend. You know why I'm the way I am. I

don't know how to put down roots…" To her horror, tears welled in her eyes and her voice wavered.

"Oh my god." Charlie scooted closer and wrapped her arms around her. "Please don't cry. I'm sorry. Please don't cry. I'm such an asshole. I just want you to be happy and self-ishly I want you to be happy here so I can have you within driving distance. Tell me about this job."

"Okay. A recruiter called me back in September about a role for a new luxury hotel group. Basically, it would be short assignments setting up concierge services and training staff before moving to another location. And the money was over the top."

Charlie's eyes narrowed. "That sounds right up your alley."

"*Oui*, at first glance it is. The recruiter even mentioned they knew I didn't have ties anywhere. But I committed to you. To everyone." A hint of unease snaked down her spine. Although she'd turned down the job offer, she had left the door open, just in case.

"So who did they end up hiring? Did you hear? Anyone we know?"

Brigitte cleared her throat. "Well, the recruiter said they were holding the position open for me until Paramount launched, in case I change my mind."

Charlie released her hands. "And you told them not to bother, right?"

Brigitte rose and paced a few steps. "I turned them down twice. She just asked if she could check in and I, well crap, I said okay. But I don't want the job. I want to stay. I just…"

"You just?" Charlie tilted her head.

"I guess I just can't totally believe this is all true. What if it doesn't work out? What happens if you and Ryan leave? Part of why I moved here is because I wanted to be close to you.

Now I want it all. So maybe it was just a back-up plan? I don't know."

"There aren't any guarantees. We both know that. You can't keep one foot out of the game and hope for the best. If you want a shot at having it all, you need to go all in."

"You're right. Because I want to stay. I want this to be forever."

"You're sure?"

"I'm sure." Her heart was racing, and her palms were damp, but she was sure.

"And what about Lucas? Do you want him forever?"

"I'm in love with Lucas and it's all so new and so different. I'm terrified."

Charlie stood and pulled her into a hug. "Oh, I get it. Falling for Ryan was the scariest time of my life. Being vulnerable? And yeah, it's hard to believe that forever is possible."

"I mean, Lucas and I haven't said "I love you" to each other yet. What happens if it doesn't work out with him?"

Charlie sat back and stared directly into her eyes. "You can have forever, okay? Even if you never have. Even if you've never found your place or your person before, you can have it now. And if Lucas is your forever, the physical place doesn't even matter, you know? I mean I love La Jolla but if Ryan wanted to start an international chain in France or Australia, that could be home, too."

"France?"

Charlie laughed. "There you are. No, no more hotels are planned. I'm just saying what I've discovered is that Ryan is home for me, no matter where we live. He's the first and the only. Do you think Lucas could be your first and only, too?"

Her heartrate accelerated. "I do. He makes me feel safe and excited at the same time. Does that make sense?"

"Absolutely. Have you told him?"

"Not yet but he has to know I'm crazy about him." Didn't he?

Charlie caught her hands and squeezed. "I'm so happy for you. And happy for me.

And you should tell him you love him. Now if you don't have any more confessions, let's get back to the party." Ah, her snarky best friend was back.

"No more confessions."

"Wonderful. I love you and everything's going to work out. Now I haven't spent this much time in a public restroom since college, even though this one's pretty fancy. I'm going to find my hot husband and have some more champagne. Come grab a glass with me?"

"Dagmar was right about the velvet bathroom couch, for sure. And yes, I'm parched after this. And thank you for being my best friend. I love you, too. Let's go."

She linked her arm through Charlie's, and they strolled back to the party.

Champagne first, then she was going to find Lucas and tell him she loved him.

BRIGITTE SIPPED the chilled Cristal and surveyed the party. Pride filled her--they'd done an incredible job with tonight's event. The hotel was gorgeous and with everything they'd created together over the past few months? It would be the most exclusive destination in Beverly Hills.

She *did* love it here and after her talk with Charlie, a sense of belonging filled her. A sense of hope she'd finally found what she'd always secretly wanted.

Nerves fluttered in her belly, but she would be brave and share everything with Lucas. Bare her heart. She'd seen the way he looked at her. Basked in his unwavering attention.

Softened in the sense of security he gave her. As if nothing could ever stop him from protecting her. She glanced at her watch.

Maybe she'd head over to the Cigar and Whiskey Lounge because he had to be almost finished with his meeting by now. She was eager for them to head up to the Penthouse Suite and begin enjoying their Romance Package.

She wove through the crowd, smiling and waving at people, eager to find Lucas.

"Brigitte."

She halted in front of a medium-sized bald man who blocked her path. "Hello, Mr...?" He looked vaguely familiar but so did half the people in the room.

"You don't remember me?" His dark eyes narrowed, and one side of his thin mouth quirked.

"I'm so sorry. We have so many people here tonight. Please refresh my memory." From where? She'd crisscrossed Los Angeles over the last few months and met countless people.

"Edward. Edward Morris. We met when you worked at the Cerulean Eden. I was very impressed with you and so here I am." He reached out a manicured hand with a large signet ring on one finger.

Was this guy for real? He'd stated his name like he was James Bond and she doubted he was a dapper spy, despite the expensive fabric of his navy suit. And she didn't recall an Edward Morris on the tightly curated guest list.

She placed her hand in his and smiled. "Well, it's nice to meet you, Mr. Morris. Welcome to Paramount. What can I do for you?"

"I won't beat around the bush. I'm the client who has been trying to hire you. Since Tracee can't seem to seal the deal with you, I flew in."

She gasped. "Pardon?" Why was he so convinced she was

the only person for the job? Was the universe trying to tell her something?

"Look, you're exactly what my company needs to excel. I want you to come on board, set up and then train concierges to be just like you. You'll stay in the most luxurious accommodations in the most exclusive cities around the world. It's the perfect lifestyle for someone like you."

Someone like her. Someone who had never settled down. Someone who didn't mind living out of a suitcase.

She rolled her shoulders back. "I'm flattered you've gone to this trouble, even though I'm not sure why you have. There are several people who would jump at this opportunity. I made myself clear to Tracee that I was happy here." Was he right? Was she really capable of being happy in one place for the first time? Was she making the biggest mistake of her life staying in Beverly Hills?

"Because I'm very particular. As we speak, my plane is at LAX and I came through Private Suite. I know you snagged an exclusive deal with them for Paramount, even though the hotel isn't open to the public yet. I need your kind of energy and drive. Name your price. Everyone has a price." He took a step closer, invading her personal space.

She held up one hand and backed up a step. This man was too much.

Before she could respond, Lucas appeared beside her, a flush on his chiseled cheekbones.

"Hello, I'm Lucas Sutton, G.M. of Paramount." His deep voice was neutral, but displeasure radiated off him in waves.

Morris nodded. "Sutton. Edward Morris."

"Excuse me but are you here as someone's guest tonight?" Lucas's voice was clipped.

Morris smirked and shook his head. "Sorry, I'm crashing your party. I flew in from Brussels to convince Brigitte to accept my offer."

Brigitte hissed out a breath. "I told your agent no. I'm sorry but you're wasting your time."

Lucas inhaled sharply but stayed silent.

Morris frowned and shook his head. Arrogant bastard. "I can't believe you're turning this opportunity down. I won't ask a fourth time."

Fury filled her but she managed to respond in a civilized manner. "The answer is no. Please don't ask again. Good night."

He stared at her for a beat, pivoted on his heel, and stalked away.

"Good riddance." She shook her head and turned toward Lucas.

His jaw was clenched. "Care to explain just what opportunity?"

She pressed one hand to his chest, but he retreated a step. "Lucas, I was going to tell you about it tonight. Let's go upstairs and I'll explain."

He gave a sharp shake of his head. "No, I want to know what's going on. That guy shows up here at an invitation-only event and says name your price and he won't ask a fourth time? What the hell is going on?"

"Let's go somewhere more private because I want to tell you--"

"Tell me here." His nostrils flared.

"I didn't tell you about it because I turned them down, okay? A recruiter called me back in September about a concierge job which was basically a series of six month assignments setting up concierge services for the hotel group."

"So why was that guy here if you turned them down? Do you know him?"

She shook her head. "I've never met him before. The recruiter didn't tell me his name. I have no idea why he thought showing up here would change my mind. I made it clear that my intention was to stay."

"Well, apparently you weren't that convincing because people don't just fly thousands of miles unless they believe they have a chance of getting what they want."

She blew out a breath and looked into his eyes, willing him to see her sincerity. "Look, I didn't think it was important to tell you since I said no. I'm sorry."

His green eyes were like chilled chips of glass. "What else haven't you told me? You didn't take that job, but you're fielding other offers or you've got a different one lined up? I mean, sticking around isn't your strong suit."

A stab of pain pierced her heart. *Direct hit.* "No, Lucas. I want to stay here. At Paramount. In Beverly Hills. With you. If we can just go upstairs, we can discuss this privately."

"How am I supposed to trust you? That guy wouldn't have shown up and told you to name your price unless he thought he had a good chance of you taking the job." He crossed his arms across his broad chest.

A flare of anger shot up her spine. She was trustworthy. "I'm telling you the truth and I'm insulted you don't believe me. I'm here, aren't I? You heard me turn him down--I can't control other people's behavior. What will it take for you to listen?"

"You know what, I need some time to process all of this. You can have the room tonight. I'm not feeling the romance." Lucas pivoted on his heel and strode away.

She pressed her hand to her throat and fought for composure. What now?

CHAPTER 23

"Great match, mate. You were an animal out there today." Steve a.k.a. Savage smacked Lucas on the back with his meaty hand.

Lucas rolled his shoulders, which had taken a beating during the eighty-minute rugby match. "Thanks. You, too." His muscles screamed but his mind was blessedly blank for the first time since Friday night.

"See you at practice next week, have a good one." Savage strode toward the makeshift bleachers where a lanky blonde beckoned him over.

The man's wife was half his size. She was one of several wives and girlfriends who religiously attended their club team matches. He'd never had a woman come to see him but today, his brothers were piling off the stands heading his way.

The guys had insisted on staying through Sunday and attending his match this morning. By now, they all had heard various versions of what had happened with Brigitte, and he appreciated them rallying around him.

"I swear, you could be in one of those superhero movies––mild-mannered accountant in the office and beast on the field." Jack high-fived him.

Lucas snorted. Jack never failed to make him laugh, even when he was feeling beat down.

"Yeah, that was impressive. I ordered us lunch and it should arrive at your place in about twenty. Let's get back because I'm starving." Austin slung an arm around his shoulder and together they headed out of the park.

"Same. I appreciate it. Appreciate you guys staying an extra day." Despite feeling pretty fucking bleak about how things went down with Brigitte, his heart warmed. His friends were always there for him.

Cam nodded. "Always, man. No matter what. Want me to ride with you?"

He had driven separately to warm up with the team. "Sure, that'd be cool."

It wasn't far to his Brentwood condo but L.A. traffic was notoriously unpredictable and today it was bumper to bumper. Neither Cam nor he were the most talkative guys, so he flipped on one of his boxing workout playlists.

"Woah, so that's the mood today, huh?" Cam side-eyed him as Linkin Park's "Crawling" blasted out in surround sound.

Yeah, maybe not the most uplifting song but their unique sound resonated, especially right now. Because he definitely wasn't feeling optimistic.

He grunted.

Cam blew out a breath and angled toward him. "Okay, so I suck at expressing feelings and stuff but if you want to talk, I'm here."

Fortunately they were at a red light because he whipped his head so fast toward his old friend, he would have plowed into the bumper in front of him. "Did you, Major Cameron Taylor, just volunteer to *talk*? About *feelings?*"

"Hey, what can I say. Lucy doesn't let me get away with brooding too long. So, yeah. And we're in the vault--just you, me, and the late great Chester Bennington."

Lucas ran his tongue around his teeth. "It's the damn *Twilight Zone*. The weekend has been intense. So, did Ryan tell you?"

"Yeah."

"About the job or about Brigitte?"

Cam nodded. "Yeah."

"This is you talking?" Lucas barked out a laugh.

His friend's lips twitched. "Okay, I'm not going to touch the situation with Brigitte because I don't know her well and I don't really know what's the deal with you two. The guys will ambush you at your place about her. Just be happy that Jon had to drive back to San Diego today, so at least it's only four to one."

He ignored the sharp ache in his chest. "Good to know. So I've got ten minutes to prepare for that. And about the G.M., I'm sorry I--"

"Do not apologize. I'm proud of you."

"Proud? How's that?"

"I'm damn proud of you. Look, you were a successful CPA, then you've handled the finances for the hotel chain for the last few years, while helping the rest of us. You're a grown man and if you want to take on a different role in the company, do it. It doesn't change that we're all equal partners, okay?"

Lucas exhaled an unsteady breath. "You don't know how much I needed to hear that. But I feel like I'm letting you guys down. We made a pact."

Cam waved a hand. "Come on. We were kids. If I hadn't gotten my leg blown off overseas, do you think I would have come back? Hell no. I loved being active military. And it's the only thing I'd ever done before the hotels. You established a successful career and one that is really damn important to the company. So I'm proud you had the balls to admit it and take a stand."

A burst of fresh energy coursed through him. "Thanks. That means a lot coming from you. And I know I've said it before but I'm sorry things didn't turn out how you'd envisioned."

Cam had lost the lower half of his leg and now used a prosthetic. He'd drifted through a dark period but taking over Cypress Coast Ranch had given him new purpose and also reunited him with his first and only love.

"Yeah, it sucks. But it meant I came home and gave me a second chance with Lucy. Life has a way of working out."

Lucas glanced over at his brother. "You must have been a hell of a leader over there. And you're doing a great job in Monterey."

"Thanks. And for what it's worth, you've kicked ass at Paramount. But you know life is too short to spend it doing something unless you're all in."

Since they'd both expressed more feelings in a twenty minute drive than they had in the last few decades, they listened to music until Lucas parked at the curb outside his building.

Ryan, Jack, and Austin pulled up behind them. They tumbled out of the car and headed up to his place. Hopefully, the rest of the guys understood and approved of his decision, too. Everyone grabbed bottles of microbrew and he took a quick shower because after this morning's game, he was ripe.

"There he is. Lunch is here. I got you a Reuben and a Club because I figured you'd need the calories after that game. Hell, my bones hurt just from watching some of those hits.

You guys are nuts." Austin shook his head and bit into a sandwich the size of his face.

He accepted the beer from Jack, grabbed the Reuben, and settled on the open spot on the end of his couch. A quick memory flashed of bending Brigitte over the arm of the couch, her long legs spread wide, her eyes heavy-lidded, and her lips parted.

He hissed out a breath and downed a mouthful of beer. Everywhere he'd looked since he'd stormed home Friday night reminded him of her. Sitting close to him, her expressive face somber as she shared her childhood stories. Leaning on the kitchen island, her head thrown back laughing at something he'd said. And he'd need to get his bathroom remodeled because his shower was ruined forever.

Damn it, he'd been planning on telling her he loved her Friday night. He'd believed she was the one. He'd started to believe that he'd found his soul mate, just like his best friends had.

But no. He'd always been a little different. So now he wouldn't run his own hotel and he wouldn't marry Brigitte.

It sucked.

"Hey, earth to Lucas. Did you hear what I said?" Jack raised his dark eyebrows.

He shook his head. "Sorry. What?"

"I said, awesome job on the soft launch. It was a great night."

He forced a small smile. "Thanks." The beginning of the night had been awesome. The end? Not so much.

"Okay, I've been nominated to say we're all cool with you switching to CFO. Hell, if I'd liked being an attorney, maybe I would have considered returning to it once Maison du Soleil opened. So don't stress. We're cool." Jack gave him a thumbs up.

"You heard my opinion." Cam toasted him with his beer.

The Michaels brothers chimed in, "We're cool." Ryan and Austin held up their beers.

"Thanks, guys. I feel good about it and think I can serve Hotel Kings best from the finance side. So are we promoting Jon?" Although Brigitte would be amazing, she'd made it pretty damn clear she didn't want more responsibility. Hell, for all he knew, she'd already bailed.

Ryan turned to him. "We don't need to discuss that right now. And since I'm the sensitive one in the group, I'm going to ask about Brigitte. What's the deal?"

Once the howling and laughter died down––because Ryan Michaels wasn't exactly known for his sensitivity–– Lucas set down his beer.

"I'm not really comfortable discussing it."

Jack rolled his eyes. "Oh for fuck's sake. What's going on? You two seemed pretty happy together. What happened? Ryan said it was something about her taking another job?"

He sighed. They wouldn't relent so he might as well share. "Yeah, I'm an idiot. Look, I've been crazy about her since your and Charlie's wedding, even though I didn't really know her. She's kind of skittish about relationships and commitment so we've taken it slow. Which worked out because I didn't want to screw up the pre-launch and you all know how much time that takes." He took a swig of beer.

"So to find out she'd been entertaining another job offer? Hell, job offers for all I know, while I'm thinking she's the one. She had one foot out the door the whole time."

"But Charlie said she'd turned down the offer. So doesn't that mean she was staying?" Ryan asked.

He threw up a hand. "She did. But that's not the point. We'd been sharing a lot of stuff and I thought she was happy here. Happy with me. I just think maybe she's afraid she can't settle down and I don't know how to make her see that."

Nobody said anything for a few moments.

"Look man, none of us are perfect. You two are pretty new. You need to have this conversation with her. Tell her you love her. Tell her you believe in her. If you really love her, you don't want to let her go.

"Because you'll regret it and question yourself unless you make damn sure you've tried everything to make it work. But if you don't love her..." Jack shrugged a shoulder and sipped his beer.

His chest tightened. "I love her. But I'm not ready to talk to her yet, okay? I need to work through it in my head."

"Yeah, but love doesn't add up like numbers in columns. It's messy. And you two are opposites, like me and Kenzie. On paper it makes no sense but in real life, it just works. Don't let that stubborn-ass ginger streak of yours push her away." Austin said.

"Yeah, it's my fault because I'm a redhead." He snorted.

"It's not your fault, okay. She's with Charlie today." Ryan leaned forward, his fingers steepled under his chin. "Look, I hate to bring it up but we've got to think about Paramount, too. I still think she'd be perfect as Assistant G.M. If she wants the job, I'm going to offer it to her and promote Jon. Is that going to be an issue?"

Yeah, this was messy. "Of course not. I hadn't thought that far ahead because I'll stay in place for however long it takes to make a smooth transition. Maybe I'd work partially remote and go to Paramount a few days a week?"

"On the professional side, I'm good with that. But you need to clear the air with her, whatever the end result, so I can talk to her about the position. Okay?"

He scrubbed his hands across his face. "Yeah, of course. Give me a couple days, okay?"

"Of course." Ryan picked up his beer. "Now that's settled, let's watch some football and chill."

Lucas reclined back into the cushions. He'd shove these

uncomfortable emotions into the vault until after the guys left. He'd enjoy being with his brothers, then allow himself to wallow tonight. He'd return her calls, but he wasn't ready. Not yet.

He would deal with the rest tomorrow.

CHAPTER 24

*B*rigitte closed her eyes, allowing the sound of the waves crashing on the golden sand to wash over her. Charlie had insisted on driving them up to Zuma Beach, claiming the ocean cured everything. And of course, her brilliant best friend was always right. Between the warming rays of the sun and the kiss of the salty breeze, her system was starting to level out.

Although her uneasy stomach and pounding temples hadn't dissipated yet.

After Lucas had stormed out of Paramount, she'd retreated to her apartment. No way could she have stayed overnight in the suite they'd planned to share. Where she'd planned to tell him she loved him. She couldn't shake the memory of Lucas's icy expression. He'd looked at her like she was a stranger, not the woman he'd professed to be falling for.

She rubbed her hand against her breastbone––was it possible that a heart could truly break? Because right now her chest hurt.

"Hey sweetie, I'm back from my walk. Feel any better yet?" Charlie dropped down next to her on the blanket they'd laid out.

She turned. "It's definitely helping. You know how much I love the water. But I hate this limbo. I know if we just have a conversation, we can clear the air. I don't want this all to be some miscommunication like in those romance novels you love so much."

"Hey, don't knock my books. Miscommunication is realistic! Just not for more than a few chapters, max. Look, Lucas is one of those people who lives a lot in his head. I've seen how he looks at you and it's obvious he's in love with you. Let his head catch up to his heart. He's hurt."

Brigitte flicked a hand. "He hasn't told me he loves me. What if he doesn't? And if he does, can I live up to his expectations? Sometimes I'm scared I'm just like my *maman*––I'm not wired to be happy in one place. Maybe it would be easier if I move on." The ache in her chest intensified.

"First of all, that's bullshit. You are wired to be happy, but you just hadn't found the place and the person until now. You said you were feeling at home in Beverly Hills and with our group. Staying is risky and can be really tough, but it's worth it.

"If you really love him, he's worth it so give him a little space. Guys retreat to their caves when their feelings are involved. And I suspect he's had feelings for you for a long time."

Her throat tightened. "I do love him. And I have been feeling at home. I don't feel restless like I usually get."

"Well, back in Miami and the Turks and Caicos, you were restless almost right away, so that's good, right? " Charlie smiled encouragingly.

"That's true. But you didn't see how he looked at me. It was like the man I'd fallen in love with didn't recognize me.

Like he was looking at a stranger he didn't particularly like." Her vision blurred and she dropped her head into her hands.

Charlie squeezed her shoulder and leaned in closer. "That's him in self-protective mode. He's going to call and all you can do is share how you feel. After that, you'll know what to do. And selfishly, I want you to stay either way."

She lifted her head, studied the indigo line of the horizon and clusters of cottony clouds. "I need to move. Can we walk?"

Maybe getting out of her head would help because right now, she didn't know what to do. If she ran, she'd disappoint her best friend. If she left, she'd fall back into her pattern of leaving when she got bored, or things got too complicated.

Charlie rose, extended one hand, and tugged her to her feet. "We can walk for miles. And there's a great café on the beach we can drive to and have a late lunch or a cocktail after, okay?"

Walking on the beach always cleared her mind and soothed her nerves. Although she wouldn't be able to settle her nerves until she'd spoken with Lucas.

BRIGITTE STOOD at her office window, taking a moment to breathe between appointments and phone calls. It was Friday afternoon and Lucas, that stubborn man, hadn't spoken to her yet. Granted, he had texted her on Sunday evening and asked if their discussion could wait until the weekend.

What could she do––they were a few weeks away from the Grand Opening Gala on New Year's Eve and they were both clocking in ridiculously long hours. Of course she would respect his request even though each day that passed made it seem less likely things would work out.

Her phone rang and Ryan's name popped up on the

screen. She hadn't spoken to him since the disastrous evening at Paramount.

"Hi, Ryan."

"We need to talk." That was Charlie's husband, Mr. Brusque.

"Of course. I've got an appointment in twenty minutes but I'm free now." She returned to her desk and sank into her comfy chair.

"Okay, I think you're doing a great job but I'm hoping you'll want to step up. I'll tell you the same thing I told Jon. Both of you would be excellent G.M.s. Jon has been training for it and wanting it since I've known him. But if you want to apply for the position, I think you'd be excellent for Paramount. Either way, I'd like you two in the G.M. and Assistant G.M. roles. What do you think?"

Her breath caught in her throat. "Oh, I wasn't expecting that." Of course she'd assumed Jon would step into Lucas's role, but she had not assumed Ryan would offer her the G.M. position.

"Well, you know Lucas is transitioning to CFO. I think you're a natural for management. But I need to know if this is what you want and if you're committed to staying. If you'd be willing to sign a two-year contract."

Brigitte squeezed her eyes closed and inhaled a fortifying breath. Staying in Beverly Hills was one thing. But a two-year contract? She didn't do contracts.

Each night this week when she'd finally collapsed into bed, her mind had raced. Questioning herself. Seeking answers. What she really desired on every level--professional and personal. Contemplated what she wanted her life to look like. Because Lucas's face popped up in every scenario, she'd forced herself to omit him from the equation because who knew if they would get back together

Spending each night alone instead of with Lucas gave her time to look at what she valued most. And planting roots in Beverly Hills, Lucas or no Lucas, ticked a lot of boxes. She loved Paramount and everyone who worked there. The small community had a European flair which resonated.

Charlie was a two hour drive away and they'd committed on carving out regular visits. And she wanted a relationship like her best friend had with Ryan.

She wanted Lucas.

She wanted it all.

"Brigitte." Impatience laced through Ryan's voice.

"Sorry, I wasn't expecting this offer. Especially with the contract. Did the other G.M.s sign contracts?"

Ryan huffed out a breath. "No, because we're the ones who started the chain together. Jon is fine with it."

As long as he wasn't singling her out because he doubted her staying power.

"Okay, I think Jon is much more experienced, especially after working directly with you. I would be happy to accept the Assistant G.M. position. But we will negotiate terms for an agreement." She pressed one hand to her roiling belly.

"Excellent. You're officially promoted. We'll figure out the timetable but I'm shooting for January. Does that work?"

Hope fluttered inside her. "It does. And Ryan?"

"Yes?"

"Thank you. I appreciate your confidence in me, despite…" She bit her lip. No, she didn't want to ask about Lucas.

"Despite?"

Oh *merde*. "Despite what happened at the soft launch and despite Lucas. We'll be professionals."

Ryan's deep voice softened. "I would expect nothing less. Does that mean you two haven't worked things out?"

She smoothed a strand of hair off her forehead. "He wanted to wait until this weekend so, no, we haven't spoken yet."

Ryan barked out a laugh. "That guy might be the most stubborn of all of us. He's crazy about you."

"Hmmm."

"Do you want some advice?"

She smoothed back a strand of hair and sighed. "Absolutely."

"Show up for him and convince him you're here to stay. I think he can't believe someone like you would fall for someone like him."

She pressed her hand to her heart. "What does that even mean?"

"You're like my wife. A force of nature, gorgeous, smart, independent, sophisticated. You two are intimidating as hell. I pinch myself every day that she chose me, especially after how we used to fight. So give him a little break about how he's handling this situation."

Her cheeks flushed at Ryan's words. "Oh, Ryan. You're perfect for my best friend. And I've never met anyone like Lucas. Thank you. Any suggestions besides clearing the air?"

Ryan chuckled. "Well, I could tell him you're signing a contract, but I don't think you want that."

"*Non,* he needs to trust my word, not demand written proof." Brigitte tapped one finger against her lips. "Thank you for helping me. I'll figure something out."

"I want my best friend to be happy and hell, I bet money on the two of you being a couple, so get out there and fix it."

Brigitte grinned. "This silly bet. Okay, I need to leave for my meeting now."

"I'm glad you accepted the new role--you and Jon will be great together. Good luck with Lucas."

Brigitte closed her eyes for a moment and pondered how

she could convince Lucas she was in Beverly Hills for good. The perfect idea flashed in her mind, and she jumped up from the chair. She had some work to do before tomorrow.

Time to find Jon, enlist his help, and swear him to secrecy.

CHAPTER 25

*L*ucas dropped into a runner's lunge, stretching out his hamstrings and hip flexors before the match. Last night's punishing run hadn't been his smartest move because now his legs were extra tight. But after last weekend, exercise helped clear his mind, but he couldn't work out 24/7.

"You ready?"

He glanced up, shading his eyes from the sun's glare. "Yeah, just warming up."

"Three minutes to line up. We're going to kick their ass today." His teammate, Rocky, who was ripped like his namesake, pumped his fist.

"I'll be there in one." Ready to burn off a ton of energy, sore legs notwithstanding.

Today was the day he'd see Brigitte. Should he have talked to her sooner? Maybe. But things were hectic at Paramount so close to opening, and he'd needed to compartmentalize to function.

Now that he'd had the week to cool off, he realized maybe he'd overreacted. He wasn't proud of his temper, but hey, he wasn't perfect. And she'd become so important to his happiness so fast--it scared the shit out of him. Because she wasn't perfect either and she'd admitted she left when she got bored.

Everyone knew accountants were boring. And he'd doubled down on it by choosing to return to a straight finance position. She was one of a few people, besides his friends and parents, he hadn't felt boring around.

Bottom line he'd acted from a place of fear. Tonight he'd man up if it wasn't too late. Hell, maybe his stubbornness to make her wait a week had pushed her away. Hell, for all he knew, she was packing her bags.

"Big Red, get your ass out here." One of his teammates shouted.

Time to stop wallowing. He surged to his feet and jogged onto the grass field. Time to kick off and kick the other team's ass. Bring it on.

The next thirty-eight minutes were a blur of sprinting and blocking and shit-talking. Or shit-shouting. It was perfect. The sun beat down on his shoulders, his heart pumped, and his mind had one focus--winning. Two minutes before the half ended, he scored. Satisfaction filled him.

The fans in the bleachers roared their approval. 1-0 and he'd put up the point. Hell, yes. He joined his team on the sidelines and grabbed a bottle of water, chugging half in one gulp.

"Hey, man. Who's the hot little brunette wearing your jersey?" Matt, one of the Forwards, asked.

Lucas stiffened. "What?" His jersey?

While all the other guys regularly had their significant others attend matches, he never had. Last weekend had been a surprise when his buddies came to the match. But he usually didn't even look over at the stands because what was the point? He played because he loved the game, plain and simple. Although sometimes it bummed him out that he didn't have his own personal cheering section.

Matt pointed toward the stands and Lucas's jaw dropped. Because there, in the front row was a hot little brunette wearing Number 7 and she was waving at him.

And not just any hot little brunette.

He blinked to make sure it was really her. A flicker of excitement shot down his spine.

It was really Brigitte. She was here.

Matt slapped his back. "What's wrong with you, dude? Get over there. We've only got eight more minutes until the second half."

He shoved his sweaty hair back from his face and jogged toward the bleachers. Brigitte stepped forward and held up an enormous sign which read, in glittering red letters, *"Je t'aime pour toujours* Lucas."

He broke into a run, and she strolled toward him, sexy as sin.

"You're here?" His throat tightened.

Her red lips curved into a wide smile. "I'm here for you."

"You're wearing my jersey." And she'd knotted the bottom of it so somehow it looked stylish. Only Brigitte.

"You're very observant today." She arched one groomed eyebrow. "What else do you see?"

"You made a sign for me?" His heart thundered against his ribs.

"Oui." She waved one elegant hand in front of the posterboard.

"Will you translate it for me?" He was pretty sure what 'Je t'aime" meant but he wanted to be sure.

"Come closer and I will tell you." Her lips curved into a wicked grin.

When they were mere inches apart, so close he caught her

unique citrusy scent, he stopped. "Does it mean you like me?" Although he was pretty sure it wasn't. But he wanted the words.

She stepped in, placed one hand on his shoulder, and gestured for him to lower his head. "I do like you. But it means I love you forever," she whispered in his ear.

Joy raced through him. With a whoop, he wrapped her in his arms, picked her up, and spun around. "Yes."

She giggled and smacked his shoulder. "Yes? That's what you say to me? Yes?"

He laughed. "Yes, yes, you've just made me the happiest man in the world. I love you, Brigitte."

He released her and slid his hands into her silky dark hair, tugged her head back and stared into her warm blue eyes. "I love you forever."

She wrapped her arms around his neck, pressed her sweet curves against him, her lips parting. He captured her mouth, sinking into her passionate, fiery response. She moaned and arched against him. Everything but Brigitte faded away.

"Hey Big Red, you've got four minutes to half. Wait until after the game and get a room, already. You've got a freakin' hotel." One of his teammates called.

He flipped them off with one hand but lifted his head. Brigitte's eyes were heavy-lidded, her cheeks pink. "Brigitte, I'm so sorry how I reacted last week. I--"

She pressed one finger against his lips. "Shh. I am sorry and we need to talk, but not here. Before you go back on the field, I wanted to tell you I accepted the Assistant G.M. position and Jon is taking G.M."

"You're staying." Could his heart burst out of his chest? Because right now, it was beating fast enough to explode.

She nodded. "I'm staying in Beverly Hills. And I want to be with you. I thought we could stay in the Penthouse tonight so we could have our Romance Package evening. We can talk through everything there, but I know my heart, and this is where I want to be. Okay?"

He picked her up again, pressed his mouth to hers. "More than okay. But I still have three minutes and I need to tell you something. I fell for you in Monterey and--"

"Monterey?" She gasped.

"Monterey." He grinned and kissed her again. "I knew from the moment we danced together, and you kissed me on the cheek that I was a goner. I knew I was crazy about you right then. I've spent these last months waiting for you to catch up. To fall as deeply in love with me as I am with you. Your strength, your courage, your joy for life blow me away. I feel like I'm my best self with you and--"

"Big Red, get your ass over here now!" Rocky bellowed.

Brigitte smacked him on his ass and stepped back with a wicked grin. "You heard the man. Now go win this game. I love you and I'll be in the stands waiting for you."

He grinned and ran back. Forty more minutes until he had her to himself. Forever.

EPILOGUE

Paramount Opening Night Gala, New Year's Eve

LUCAS AND BRIGITTE stood together at the entrance of the Whiskey and Cigar Lounge and surveyed the festive, lively crowd filling Paramount's lobby. From chic celebrities to opening night hotel guests to Beverly Hills Mayor, the party buzzed with conversations and upbeat tunes spun by a local DJ. Glittering lights adorned the high-ceilinged space and waitstaff circulated with flutes of champagne.

"It's absolutely perfect. The best opening gala yet." Brigitte murmured in her throaty voice, sending sparks racing down his spine.

He pulled her closer and kissed her soft red lips. This incredible woman loved him, and he'd never been happier. And tonight marked the opening of the fifth and final luxury boutique hotel in the chain, and it exceeded his expectations.

"I couldn't have done it without you. Why don't you give

the welcome toast?" Maybe she was so head-over-heels for him she'd save him the pain of public speaking tonight.

She pressed one elegant hand to his chest. "*Non*, you and Jon should do it. You as the original G.M. and Jon as the new one. Remember, you don't have to give a long speech, just speak from the heart."

His heart kicked, just like it did every time she touched him, and he sipped his champagne. "Speak of the devil. Here comes everyone. Hell, maybe Ryan will do it."

The entire Hotel Kings family joined them. Ryan and Charlie bickering and laughing, Jack and Campbell with their arms wrapped around each other, Cam and Lucy holding hands and smiling, Austin and Kenzie somehow kissing as they walked, and Jon with his date, who happened to be one of Lucas's rugby teammates.

"Lucas is trying to convince me or Ryan to give the toast." Brigitte flashed him her wicked grin. The little traitor.

Ryan pointed at him. "No way. Jon and Brigitte, you can say a few words, too, if you want but this is Lucas's baby, even if he's handing it off. Without your vision and your dedication, Paramount wouldn't be the success it is already. And, I'm saying this as your boss and your friend."

Satisfaction filled him even as heat rose on the back of his neck. Yeah, his best friend wouldn't let him slide out of this as easily as he'd agreed to let him step down.

"Lucas, you give the speech. And maybe you can thread in something about how every hotel opening coincides with a love story?" Jon winked.

Lucy clapped her hands together. "Yes, I think that's the best part. You guys exceeded the vision for the business you dreamed up all those years ago. And as our wedding planner, I find it incredibly romantic that each of you found true love."

Jack smirked. "It is romantic, even though your cranky

bastard of a fiancé mocked me and said my proposal to his sister was like a Hallmark movie."

Campbell laughed and elbowed her brother. "Yeah Cam, Jack's proposal was perfect. And your and Lucy's story is definitely a movie-of-the-week."

"You know, maybe I can add that to our Sales and Marketing literature--stay at one of the Hotel Kings' luxury hotels and maybe you'll find true love." Charlie grinned, her dark eyes twinkling.

Kenzie looked up at Austin. "And Austin could write the theme song. I still think he or Ryan should ask their dad to use his show business ties for a reality show or even a limited television series."

"Yes." Charlie hooted. "We've got all the best tropes--enemies to lovers, forced proximity, second chance, big brother's best friend, and opposites attract for Austin and Kenzie and you and Brigitte. It's perfect."

Ryan shook his head. "Don't look at me. I mean, Chris and my mom are here tonight. Knock yourself out but I'm not asking."

"Me, either. And it's too late for a reality show anyway; Paramount is our last hotel and we're all already paired up," Austin said.

Lucas held up both hands. "Rein it in, people. It's the Opening Gala. If it will get you to stop this spiral into bad television, I'll say a few words. Austin, can you use your lung power to get everyone's attention?"

Austin grinned. "Fine but I'm not singing tonight, you've already got the DJ spinning tunes." He pivoted to face the party and used his lead singer vocals. "Beverly Hills. Can I have your attention over here, please? It's time for a toast."

The crowd quieted and turned toward them. Go time. Brigitte laced her fingers with his and squeezed.

Lucas swallowed the nerves bubbling up in his throat.

"Thank you all so much for celebrating our grand opening with us tonight. As many of you know, Paramount is the fifth boutique hotel my colleagues and I have opened in California over the last two years. We picked cities that are different and unique––La Jolla, Paso Robles, Monterey, Palm Springs, and finally here, our special little town of Beverly Hills. We hope you have a fantastic time tonight and return year after year.

"If you're local, join us in our Whiskey and Cigar Lounge or Belcanto, which promises to be an award winning restaurant, anytime. It's New Year's Eve so we'll have our own version of a ball drop and endless champagne. We couldn't do this out without your support, so thank you."

Cheers, toasts, and applause filled the expansive space.

"Congrats to all of us. We pulled this off and I'm proud to be a part of it." Cam raised his glass.

"To us." They tapped glasses and drank.

Campbell caught Jack's hand. "Jack owes me a dance, anybody else coming?"

They had set up a small dance floor near the reception desk. Which gave Lucas an idea.

He turned to Brigitte. "Will you dance with me?"

Her beautiful red lips curved upward. "Of course. Last time we danced I had to drag you onto the dance floor. Let's do it."

He nodded and they wove through the throngs of guests to where other couples were swaying to slow ballad. Perfect. He wouldn't even have to ask the DJ to play a slow song. They found a sliver of space and he drew Brigitte close, wrapping his arms around her waist.

She wound her arms around his neck and gazed up at him, her slate blue eyes heavy-lidded. "Tonight has been wonderful. I'm so proud of you."

His heart tugged in his chest. "Thank you. Brigitte, I fell

for you in Monterey. I never thought my crush would take us here but now that you're mine, I never want to let you go. You're a shining light and I'm so lucky to be in your orbit. You're so clever and witty and confident--you make me smile every single day. I want you to know that I'm yours. I've got your back--I love you and I want to spend every day living in the present moment with you, for the rest of my life."

Her eyes were wide, her face soft. "Lucas. I don't know what I did to deserve you, but I am yours and you are mine. I never believed I'd find my true home and I have in you. I love you so much."

She dug her fingers into his hair and tugged his head down. "Let's seal it with a kiss."

He slanted his mouth across hers, savoring her sweet taste, and joy welled up in his heart.

Hands linked, they stepped off the dance floor to celebrate tonight and the first night of forever.

WHAT'S NEXT

Thanks so much for reading *Beverly Hills King*! I hope you loved Lucas and Brigitte's story. If you have a moment, please leave a review for *Beverly Hills King* on your favorite book site.

If you haven't read the series, start with Book 1:
Hotel King today!
****

To see the series where it all started before California Suits, check out the Pacific Vista Ranch series here:
https://clairemarti.com/book_series/pacific-vista-ranch/

ALSO BY CLAIRE MARTI

Pacific Vista Ranch Series

Nobody Else But You

The Very Thought of You

For The Love of You

Wrapped Up with You

The Wonder of You

California Suits Series

Hotel King

Wine Country King

Monterey King

Holiday Queen

Palm Springs King

Beverly Hills King

True Stars Collide (related novella)

Romance in Laguna Beach Series

Second Chance in Laguna

At Last in Laguna

Sunset in Laguna

ACKNOWLEDGMENTS

It's a bittersweet feeling to finish the California Suits series. I've been in this world with my Hotel Kings for more than two years now. Actually, five years, because we met Ryan and Austin Michaels back in Pacific Vista Ranch before they inspired this spin-off series. It's been a blast having (cough cough) to visit all these beautiful towns in California, which are now some of my favorite places.

Thanks to all the readers who shared how they felt transported to La Jolla, Paso Robles, Monterey, Palm Springs, and now Beverly Hills. I'm happy to provide the escape! Thank you to all the readers who read my books! I love writing them and as long as you keep reading…I'll keep going! Thank you for allowing me to live my dream.

I want to thank my wonderful beta readers: Donna Simonetta, Kay Bennett, Joanna Kelly, and Sara Martin—I couldn't do this without your helpful and insightful feedback! For the lovely author friends I've made along the way, with whom I share such a sense of camaraderie, thanks for being there: Christina Hovland, Serena Bell, Kerrigan Byrne, Katie O'Sullivan, Donna Simonetta and so many more.

To my wonderful editor, Lindsey Faber, thank you for your consistently excellent suggestions, keen insight, brilliant ideas, and the way you push me to make each story better. Thank you to Shasta Schafer for your skillful proof-reading. Thank you Sarah Paige for the beautiful covers you create.

Last but not least, to Todd for being the best husband in the world. I love you. And, finally to my furry kids: Lola, Beau, Josie, and Daisy thanks for providing me daily laughs and all the cuddles.

ABOUT THE AUTHOR

Claire Marti is an award winning and *USA Today* Bestselling author of swoonworthy Contemporary Romance novels set in Southern California, including the California Suits series, Pacific Vista Ranch series, and the Romance in Laguna Beach series. She lives in San Diego with her husband, silly dog, and three clever cats.

Claire started writing stories as soon as she was old enough to pick up pencil and paper. After graduating from the University of Virginia with a BA in English Literature, Claire was sidetracked by other careers, including practicing law, selling software for legal publishers, and managing a non-profit animal rescue for a Hollywood actress.

Finally, Claire followed her heart and now focuses on two of her true passions: writing romance and teaching yoga.

www.ingramcontent.com/pod-product-compliance
Lightning Source LLC
Chambersburg PA
CBHW021154310726
48971CB00002B/630